Foxglove Tales

Alison Uttley was born in 1884 and this collection of stories was published to celebrate her centenary.

Five of them come from *Moonshine and Magic*, the first and perhaps the most delightful of her many volumes of stories, but the three from *Lavender Shoes,* her last book for children, show that she had not lost her skill at the age of eighty-six. Sam Pig and Tim Rabbit, the heroes of two of her most popular series, are also represented, and there are stories from *Nine Starlight Tales* and *The Weathercock.*

Alison Uttley's best stories for children combine fantasy, humour and the feeling for nature that informs all her writing. This centenary volume is exquisitely illustrated by Shirley Felts.

Also by Alison Uttley
in Piccolo

Tales of Little Grey Rabbit

Illustrated by Faith Jaques

Tales of Little Brown Mouse

Illustrated by Faith Jaques

Alison Uttley

Foxglove Tales

Chosen by Lucy Meredith

Illustrated by Shirley Felts

Piccolo Books

First published in 1984
by Faber and Faber Ltd

This Piccolo edition published
1986 by Pan Books Ltd,
Cavaye Place, London, SW10 9PG
9 8 7 6 5 4 3 2 1

ISBN 0 330 29527 6

Printed and bound in Great Britain by
Cox & Wyman Ltd, Reading

'All round our walls grew tall foxgloves, giants with families of little ones springing from the parent stem . . . They were glove fingers, which interested every country child. We walked with silky purple gloves, and we felt important, as if we touched some secret magic.'

Alison Uttley, 'Flowers', *Country Hoard*

Contents

Sam Pig
Seeks his Fortune

One day Sam Pig started out to seek his fortune, and this was the reason. He came down as usual for breakfast, with never a thought except that he was hungry and there was a larder full of food. It was a sunny morning and he decided he would bask in the garden, and enjoy himself, and do nothing at all.

'Go and fill the kettle at the spring,' said Ann, when he entered the room. He picked up the copper kettle and carried it down the lane to the spring of water which gushed out of the earth. Then he staggered slowly back, spilling all the way.

'That's my day's work done,' he said to himself as he lifted it to the fire.

'Go and chop some sticks, Sam,' said Bill, when he was comfortably settled at the table. He picked up the axe from the corner and went to the wood-stack. Then he chipped and he chopped till he had a fine pile of kindling. He filled the wood-box and brought it back to the house.

'That's two days' work done,' said he to himself as he put some of the wood under the kettle. He returned to his seat but Ann called him again.

'Blow up the fire, Sam,' she ordered. He reached down the blow-bellows and he puffed and he huffed and he blew out his own fat cheeks as well as the bellows. Then the fire crackled and a spurt of flame roared out and the kettle began to sing.

'That's three days' work done,' said Sam to himself and he listened to the kettle's song, and tried to find out what it said.

'Go and fetch the eggs, Sam,' said Tom, and away he went once more. He chased the hens out of the garden and hunted under the hedgeside for the eggs. He put them in a rhubarb-leaf basket and walked slowly back to the house. His legs were tired already, and he looked very cross.

'That's four days' work done,' said he to himself, and he put the basket on the table. Then he sat down and waited for breakfast, but Ann called him once more.

'Sam. Wash your face and brush your hair,' she said. 'How can you sit down like a piggy-pig?'

That settled it! To be called a piggy-pig was the last straw! All Sam's plans suddenly changed. His life was going to be different. He had had enough of family rule.

'I'm going to seek my fortune,' he announced loudly, when he had scrubbed his face and hands and brushed his bristly hair. 'I'm going off right away after breakfast to seek my fortune.'

He put a handful of sugar in his cup and blew on his tea and supped his porridge noisily, in defiant mood.

'And what may that be?' asked Bill sarcastically. 'What is your fortune, Sam?'

'His face is his fortune,' said Tom, rudely.

'You foolish young pig,' cried Ann. 'What would Badger say? You must stay at home and help us. We can't do without you.'

'I know you can't.' Sam tossed his head. 'That's why I'm going.' And he ate his breakfast greedily, for he didn't know when he would have another as good.

He took his knapsack from the wall and put in it a loaf of bread and a round cheese. He brushed his small hooves and stuck a feather in his hat. Then he cut a stick from the hazel tree and away he went.

'Good-bye,' he called, waving his hat to his astonished sister and brothers. 'Good-bye, I shall return rich and great some day.'

'Good-bye. You'll soon come running back, Brother Sam,' they laughed.

Now he hadn't gone far when he heard a mooing in some bushes.

'Moo! Moo! Moo!'

He turned aside and there was a poor lone cow caught by her horns, struggling to free herself. He unfastened the boughs and pulled the branches asunder so that the cow could get away.

'Thank you. Thank you,' said the cow. 'Where are you going so early, Sam Pig?'

'To seek my fortune,' said Sam.

'Then let me go with you,' said the cow. 'We shall be company.' So the cow and Sam went along together, the cow ambling slowly, eating as she walked, Sam Pig trying to hurry her.

'Take a lift on my back,' said the cow kindly, and Sam leapt up to her warm comfortable back. There he perched himself with his little legs astride and his tail curled up.

They went through woods and along lanes. Sam stared about from the cow's back, seeking his fortune everywhere.

'Miaou! Miaou!' The cry came from a tree, and Sam looked up in surprise. On a high bough sat a white cat, weeping and wailing in misery.

'What is the matter?' asked Sam.

'I've got up here,' sobbed the white cat, 'and I can't get down. I've been here for two nights and a day, and nobody has helped me. There are boogles and witches about in the night, and I'm scared out of my seven wits.'

'I'll get you down,' said Sam Pig proudly, and he stood on the cow's head and reached up with his hazel switch. The white cat slithered along it and slipped safely to the ground.

'Oh, thank you! Thank you, kind sir,' said the

cat. 'I'll go with you, wherever you go,' said she.

'I'm going to seek my fortune,' said Sam.

'Then I'll go too,' said the white cat, and she walked behind the cow with her tail upright like a flag and her feet stepping delicately and finely.

Away they went to seek Sam's fortune, and they hadn't gone far when they heard a dog barking.

'Bow wow. Bow wow,' it said.

The cow turned aside and the cat followed, after a natural hesitation.

In a field they saw a poor thin dog with its foot caught in a trap. The cow forced the trap open and released the creature. Away it limped, holding up its paw, but Sam put a dock-leaf bandage upon it, and bound it with ribbons of grasses.

'I'll come with you,' said the dog gratefully. 'I'll follow you, kind sir.'

'I'm going to seek my fortune,' said Sam.

'Then I'll go too,' barked the dog, and it followed after. But the white cat changed her place and sprang between the cow's horns; and that's the way they went, the cow with Sam on her back and the cat between her horns and the lame dog trotting behind.

Now after a time they heard a squeaking and a squawking from the hedgeside. There was a little Jenny Wren, struggling for its life in a bird-net.

'What's the matter?' asked Sam.

'I'm caught in this net and if nobody rescues

me, I shall die,' cried the trembling wren.

'I'll save you,' said Sam, and he tore open the meshes of the net and freed the little bird.

'Oh, thank you. Thank you,' said the wren. 'I'll go with you wherever you go.'

Then it saw the green eyes of the cat watching it from the cow's horns, so it flew to the other end of the cow and perched on its tail. Away they all went, the cow with the pig on her back and the cat on her horns and the bird on her tail, and behind walked the dog.

They went along the woods and meadows, always seeking Sam's fortune. After a time it began to rain and they got bedraggled and wet. Then out came the sun and they saw a great rainbow stretching across the sky and dipping down to the field where they walked. The beautiful arch touched the earth at an old twisty hawthorn tree.

'That's where my fortune is hidden,' cried Sam, pointing to the thorn bush. 'At the foot of the rainbow, Badger told me once to look there. "Seek at the foot of a rainbow and you'll find a fortune," he said to me, and there's the rainbow pointing to the ground!'

So down they scrambled: the white cat leapt from the cow's horns, Sam sidled from the cow's back and the bird flew down from the cow's tail. They all began to dig and to rootle with horns and feet and bill and claws and snout. They tossed

14

away the black earth and dug into the crumpled roots of the tree. There lay a crock filled with pieces of gold.

'Here's my fortune,' cried Sam Pig, lifting it out.

'We can't eat it,' said the cow, snuffling at it with her wet nose. 'It's hard as stone.'

'We can't eat it,' said the white cat, putting out a delicate pink tongue. 'It's tough as wood.'

'We can't eat it,' barked the dog, biting with sharp teeth at the gold. 'It's harsh as rocks.'

'We can't eat it,' sang the bird, pecking at the pieces. 'It's cruel as a snare.'

'What use is your fortune?' they all asked Sam.

'I don't know.' Sam shook his head and scratched himself behind the ear. 'I've found it, and that is what I set out to do.'

'I'm weary,' said the cow. 'Let us stay here all night.'

The cow began to crop the grass, and the cat supped the bowl of milk which the cow gave to it. The bird found a few fat worms where the earth had been disturbed. As for Sam, he shared his bread and cheese with the dog, and all were satisfied and at peace with one another. The cow tucked her legs under her big body and bowed her head in sleep. The cat curled up in a white ball. The wren put its head under its wing. The dog rested with its chin on its paws.

Then Sam cut a stick from the hawthorn tree. It

was a knobby thorn full of magic, for it had guarded the gold for a thousand years, ever since the fairies had hidden it. Of course Sam didn't know that, but Badger would have warned him if he had been there.

'Never cut a bough from a twisty ancient thorn,' he would have said. 'There's a power of magic hidden in it.'

Sam cut the thorn and trimmed it with his clasp knife, and leaned it up against the tree over the crock of gold, all ready to catch a robber if one should come in the night. Then he lay down next to the dog.

The moon came up in the sky and looked at the strange assembly under the old hawthorn tree. She blinked through the branches of the old thorn and shot her moonbeams at the cudgel, shaking it into life. Slowly it rose and staggered across the grass. Then it began to belabour every creature there except the little wren which was asleep in the tree.

When the cow felt the sharp blows across her ribs, she turned on the dog and tossed it with her sharp horns. The dog rushed at the cat and tried to worry it. The cat scrambled up the tree and tried to catch the bird. The little Jenny Wren awoke with a cry and flew away.

Sam took to his heels and ran as fast as he could along the lanes and through the woods and across the meadows till he reached home. He banged at

the door and wakened them all up.

'Where's the fortune, Sam?' asked Bill and Tom and little Ann Pig. 'Did you find a crock of gold?'

'Yes. A crock of gold,' cried Sam, out of breath with running so fast. 'A crock of gold under the rainbow end.'

'Where is it?' they asked. 'Gold is useful sometimes and it would do fine to mend the hole in our roof. Where is it, Sam?'

Then Sam told how he had found the gold under the hawthorn tree, but the tree had belaboured them soundly in the night and he had run home.

'That gold is bewitched,' said Ann. 'Best leave it where you found it.'

'I would like to see the crock of gold, and touch it, and smell it,' interrupted Bill.

'So would I,' added Tom. 'I've never seen any gold.'

'Then I will take you there tomorrow after I've had a good sleep,' yawned Sam. 'That is if you don't make me work before breakfast.'

The next morning they all went across the wood and over the meadows to the old hawthorn tree where Sam had found the crock of gold.

A cow was feeding in the thick grass of the field, and a white cat was leaning with her paw outstretched over the stream fishing for minnows. A dog chased a rabbit through the hedge and a little

18

Jenny Wren piped and sang.

There was no crock of gold anywhere to be seen, but underneath the old bent tree grew a host of king-cups, glittering like gold pence in the sunshine, fluttering their yellow petals in their dark green leaves.

'You imagined the gold,' said Bill indignantly. 'You've led us here on a wild goose chase,' and he cuffed poor Sam Pig over the head.

'I didn't!' protested Sam. 'There's the cudgel I cut from the tree.'

On the ground lay a thick stick, knotted and thorny and dark. The pigs leaned over it without touching it; then they began to gather the flowers.

'Quite true,' they nodded. 'Quite true, Sam Pig. You did find a fortune after all. There it lies, all turned into yellow flowers, much more use than metal to a family of pigs. Let the human kind take the hard metal, and we'll take the posies. King-cups are good for pains and aches; their seeds make pills and their leaves are cool poultices and their flowers are a delight to our sharp noses.'

They gathered a bunch and walked slowly home through the fresh fields wet with dew. All the way they talked to Sam kindly and treated him as if he had indeed brought a fortune to them.

'Badger will be pleased with you, little Pig-wiggin,' said they and this was high praise for little Sam Pig.

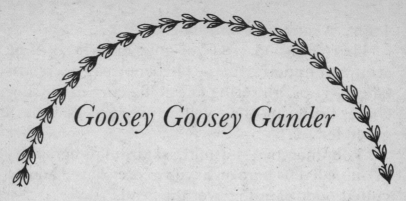

Goosey Goosey Gander

In the little whitewashed cottage with the thatched roof, and 1666 over the doorway, there once dwelt a lady. The cottage was the neatest, prettiest, best-kept house in those days, with clipped yew hedges, and violets, sweet-williams, periwinkles and cowslips growing in the little garden, among apple-trees and cherries. At the diamond-paned windows hung white lawn curtains, decked with dainty frills, all as clean as a new pin, yet no one had ever seen a servant about the place!

How did Miss Primrose manage to do all the work, yet always appear in her sprigged muslin gown and snowy mob cap, fresh as if she had stepped out of a band-box? Nobody knew.

The secret was, she had two of the very best servants in the whole countryside. They were a goose and a gander!

Every day the gander chopped the sticks, lighted the fire, cleaned Miss Primrose's buckled shoes, and swept the garden path. Every day the goose laid an egg for the lady's breakfast, and cooked it in the frying-pan. It warmed the teapot, and made the tea, it toasted the bread and put it in the silver toast rack. Then it tinkled a tiny silver bell, and called 'Ss-ss-ss-ss', and Miss Primrose came tripping down the shallow oak stairs to her little kitchen.

The stone floor was swept clean, the bowl on the linen cloth was full of roses, red and white, the windows were wide open, and the early morning sunlight came streaming in. Miss Primrose spread out the full skirt of the lavender print dress she wore in the morning, and sat down to breakfast. She was very happy and she talked to the white goose as it waddled round the room, waiting on her.

'I should like some watercress for lunch today,' said she. 'Please tell the gander, goosey dear,' and out of doors trotted the goose to the gander, who was standing by the garden hedge whispering to a crowd of quacking ducks in the field.

The gander mentioned the matter of watercress to the ducks, and away they went in an important procession to the brook. Soon they came marching back again, with their beaks filled with fresh green cresses, and the gander washed them in the water-trough by the door and took them to the kitchen.

Miss Primrose had finished her breakfast when they returned, and she went to the hedge to thank them, and repayed them with the scraps from her table. Then she tucked up her skirt, put on an apron and a frilly sunbonnet, and went out to milk her cow. She went through the white gate at the side of the cottage to the cowhouse, which was next door. She took her milking-stool from the corner of the shed, and her wooden milk-pail from a hook. Then she called her Jersey cow.

'Coo. Coo-up. Coo-up, Buttercup,' she called in a high voice, and the cow came frisking in at the door. It stood very still whilst she milked it. 'Swish! Swish!' went the milk into the bucket, and the cow turned its head and looked at her with soft eyes. It didn't mind the goose and the gander looking after its comforts, but it refused to let them milk it. Only the lady's gentle fingers could do that.

When Miss Primrose had finished, the gander came to put down fresh straw, and to give it a mouthful of hay and a drink of water before turning it out into the meadow again.

The great bird seized a brush and swept the floor, and sent an inquisitive mouse scurrying into a hole, fearful of its strong beak. Then it went back, waddling through the gate into the garden, to its weeding and hoeing and tying up of plants.

It weeded with its beak, and hoed with its foot, and dug with a little fork the lady had bought for it. The gander was a fine gardener, for it never seemed to tire, and the fruit on the trees and the flowers in the beds showed how clever it was at its work.

The little lady carried the milk back to the house, and the good goose put some aside for cream, and some to be made into cheese, and some it used for junkets and syllabubs. Then the goose and the lady made the bed, and turned down the top sheet with its embroidered edge of white poppies and wheat-ears, and put on the bedcover with its old English quilting.

Suddenly there was a knock at the door. The goose crept under the bed, and the gander strolled across the garden, and stood with an innocent air gazing at the sky to see if it would rain.

'Will it pour?' it seemed to say. 'Will it be wet today?' although it knew quite well it would be fine. The fork was tucked under its wing, nothing could be seen.

Miss Primrose ran downstairs in a flutter, and opened the door. There stood the parson.

'May I come in?' he asked in his high fluting voice, and the little lady bobbed and curtseyed. She invited him into her parlour and drew forward a chair. Then she went to the corner cupboard for cowslip wine and little heart-shaped cinnamon biscuits.

'What a charming room this is, Miss Primrose,' said he, looking round curiously, and twiddling his thumbs. 'My wife says she cannot think how you manage without a maid or man. How do you do it? Your garden is perfect, yet you never seem to work in it. Your house is exquisite, and yet you allow those geese to walk about wherever they want. How do you manage?'

Miss Primrose blushed as she poured out the golden wine into a slender glass, but she said nothing, for she knew he would be astonished if he heard about her servants.

'I suppose you are fattening your geese for Michaelmas, Miss Primrose,' continued the parson, sipping the wine. 'My wife wished me to ask you the price of the gander, as she would like you to reserve him for our Michaelmas feast.'

'Indeed no!' cried Miss Primrose, so emphatically that the clergyman stared. 'No! No! No! My geese are my friends.'

'You always have your joke,' laughed the parson. 'We all get fond of our dumb pets, but surely you intend to fatten and kill them?'

'No, sir,' protested poor Miss Primrose, blushing more than ever, and devoutly hoping that the geese couldn't hear with their sharp ears. 'They are my dearest friends. I couldn't do without them.

'You see,' she went on, desperately trying to be truthful, 'they help me in my house and garden.'

'Yes, I suppose they eat up the scraps and keep down the slugs and snails. I suppose so. Well, I'm sorry you won't part with your birds, Miss Primrose. My wife had set her heart on one of them,' said he, rising and holding out his hand. 'Good day. Good day,' and Miss Primrose curtseyed again and held open the door.

As he went down the garden path he saw the gander standing like a statue, with its beak in the air.

'A fine bird,' said he, longingly. 'Maria will be annoyed.'

The goose crept from under the bed and went on with its dusting. The little lady sighed at the deception, and sat down to her embroidery. 'Neighbours are too inquisitive,' said she to herself. 'Why shouldn't I have a goose and a gander for my servants and friends? They don't leave, they don't want wages; they don't gossip, except with the ducks and hens; they are beautiful to look upon; they are clean and clever; and I love them and they love me!'

She peeped through the window at the snowy gander, now digging in a little spot hidden by the thick yew-hedge from the eyes of chance passers-by. It was a wonderful bird for deceiving the villagers.

In the afternoon Miss Primrose dressed herself in her dainty blue muslin gown, and put on her straw bonnet with forget-me-nots and blue ribbons. She hid the key under a shell on the window-sill, and then set off with a basket to do her shopping.

The goose and the gander sauntered away together across the field to the common. It was their holiday time, and they swam on the pond, and chattered to the ducks and drakes. They walked among the turkeys and hens and guinea-fowl in the field, and talked of the lovely day, and the sunshine, and the wetness of water, and the sweetness of grass.

At four o'clock their mistress would return, and the pair kept an eye on the sun. At the correct moment they waddled back across the fields and into the house, through the tiny goose-door which was cut in the wall. Then they prepared tea for Miss Primrose.

They welcomed her with cackles of joy. The goose carried her poke bonnet upstairs and laid it in the bandbox and the gander took off her

buckled shoes and put on her velvet slippers, whilst she told it what she had seen and heard in the village.

Sometimes she sat in the garden among her roses and lilies, and the goose and the gander sat on either side of her, whilst she read aloud the amusing fables of old Mr Aesop, or the comedies of Mr Shakespeare. Sometimes she sat at her spinet in the little parlour, and the goose and the gander lay at her feet, whilst she sang sweet songs to them. Sometimes she sat by the cosy kitchen fire, with her spinning-wheel, and the goose and the gander wound the wool, and listened to the ballads which she told them of long ago.

When it was eight o'clock Miss Primrose locked the doors and went upstairs to her room. The goose followed after, to fold up her clothes, and to brush her shining hair. Then the lady knelt down and said her evening prayer, and the goose waited quietly near. It tucked the little lady safely in her bed, kissed her with a soft feathery kiss, and closed the door. The goose and the gander went to their own room, and nestled in the round beds of hay the lady had provided for them. Soon there was no sound in the pretty cottage except the ruffle of sleepy wings, and the drip drip of the water in the stone troughs.

So they went on in their uneventful life. On Sundays Miss Primrose drew on her black silk mittens and went to church, but the goose and the gander stood on the little green lawn, enjoying the sunshine and the sound of the bells. If they could have accompanied Miss Primrose, they would have gone too, but their mistress didn't think it was seemly, so they stayed quietly at home, and as they were as good as gold, perhaps it didn't matter.

When it rained, Miss Primrose took her green silk umbrella, and put on a pair of pattens – wooden shoes with iron heels, to lift her feet out of the mud – but the goose and the gander sat on the lawn with the water dripping over their backs. It was all the same to them; wet or fine, they enjoyed life.

One Sunday the little lady went to church and forgot to lock the door. Indeed, she left the key in the lock, instead of hiding it under the pearly shell on the window-sill. The goose and the gander sat on the lawn, half-dreaming of celestial ponds as they listened to the ringing bells in the village church. The cow stood under the tree in the field, swinging her tail idly, and she, too, listened to the bells. The thrushes and blackbirds sang in company.

The gate opened and an old man came into the garden. With only a glance at the startled eyes of the goose and the gander he walked up to the cottage and peered through the windows. Then he saw the key in the lock, and he turned it and walked inside.

'I'll just peep round,' said he, 'and see what kind of a house Miss Primrose has. I know she's safe at church, for I seed her go in. Nobody'll be any the wiser.'

So he walked in the parlour and kitchen, and poked his nose in the pantry and dairy. He put an egg in his pocket, and half a pound of butter. He picked up one of the white loaves the goose had baked, and bit a piece out of it.

'This tastes grand!' he exclaimed, and he ate it all and also a bowl of curds and whey which lay ready for Miss Primrose.

He tiptoed round the rooms, looking at the clock with a sun and moon on its dial, at the china dogs with chains round their necks, at the brass candlesticks and the spinet. Then he opened the door at the foot of the stairs, and walked slowly up to the bedrooms. The goose and the gander stretched their necks and stared at the open door, and listened to the footsteps wandering round the house.

'That old man ought to be in church,' said the goose to the gander. 'He ought to be saying his prayers, like our kind mistress.'

'Yes,' agreed the gander. 'Do you think he is one of those wicked ones who don't say prayers?'

They looked at each other in dismay, and waddled softly to the house, their eyes wide, their wings outstretched.

The old man opened a door on the landing.

'Does she let her geese sleep in the house like humans?' he cried aloud, astonished at the round nests with their hay mattresses and their little white sheets and yellow blankets. There was a tiny looking-glass standing on the ground, for the geese to preen themselves, and a great bowl of water with a blue bath-mat. There was a picture of the goose that laid a golden egg on the wall, and a sampler with a rhyme embroidered upon it in cross-stitch.

Amazed, he shut the door, but he did not notice the quiet flip-flip of the goose's steps following him. From room to room he went, and after him went the goose. At last he entered the lady's little white bedchamber. There was her pretty bed with its goose-feather pillow, its quilted cover, and its embroidered linen sheets, snowy as the goose that had washed them. On the wall hung the picture of an angel with great feathery wings like the gander's, and on the white scrubbed floor was a white feather mat.

The old man took off his coat and hung it on a chair. He slipped off his dirty boots, put his pipe on a table, and got into bed.

'Just time for a nap before she comes back,' he muttered, and he shut his tired old eyes and fell asleep in a moment.

'He hasn't said his prayers,' whispered the goose who stood watching him with its beady eyes. 'Gander was right after all. He's gone to bed without saying his prayers!'

It approached the bed and tugged at the sheets with its beak.

'Old man! Old man!' it hissed. 'Get up and say your prayers.'

The old man opened one eye, and looked at the goose. Then he pulled the blankets up to his chin. 'Go away, Goosey Gander,' he grumbled sleepily. 'Leave me in peace, can't you?'

The goose dragged off the clothes, and pecked him out of bed. He struggled and kicked, and it flew at him with flapping wings and fierce beak, so there was nothing for him to do but to slip on his boots and coat and leave the room as quickly as possible.

'Drat the goose!' he cried. 'What's the matter with it?'

But the goose seized him by the left leg as he went through the door, and flung him, spinning like a top, downstairs. The gander came running from the kitchen when it heard the noise.

'He didn't say his prayers,' cried the goose, breathlessly. 'Nobody gets into bed without saying their prayers, do they?'

'No,' agreed the gander, and it pecked the old man's leg to hurry him out of the house. The old man didn't need any more reminders, he scuttled away as fast as he could, and the goose and the gander put fresh sheets on the bed and tidied up the dirty marks.

Miss Primrose came tripping back from church with her prayer book in her hand. She had met an old man in the lane, who touched his hat and shuffled away when she smiled and bade him good morning. She was sorry for him, and she determined to send him a basket of eggs, when the goose had laid enough.

She went upstairs to take off her mittens and her Sunday shawl. As she smoothed her hair she looked round the room and noticed a blackened pipe lying on a table. She took it, and smiled.

She went along the passage to the goose and gander's sleeping-room and stood for a minute reading the embroidered sampler on the wall. Then she called her little servants upstairs.

With soft flipping steps they came to her, and stood on each side staring at her with wide golden eyes.

'I've never read this tale to you, have I?' asked Miss Primrose, and the goose and the gander shook their snowy heads and gazed at the criss-cross embroidery, which they had always thought to be the multiplication table, not a rhyme at all!

Then Miss Primrose read it aloud, and this is what she read:

' "*Goosey Goosey Gander*
Whither dost thou wander?"
"*Upstairs and downstairs,*
And in my lady's chamber.

There I met an old man,
Who wouldn't say his prayers.
I took him by the left leg,
And threw him downstairs." '

'Why! That's us!' cried the goose and the gander together, and they hissed with joy and excitement. At night, when the lady sat at her spinet, she sang them their own song of 'Goosey Goosey Gander', and the two geese lay at her feet, with their bright eyes fixed upon her, listening to the tinkling tune which one day would become a nursery rhyme:

' *"Goosey Goosey Gander,*
Whither dost thou wander?"
"Upstairs and downstairs,
And in my lady's chamber.
There I met an old man,
Who wouldn't say his prayers.
I took him by the left leg,
And threw him downstairs." '

The Fox and the Little White Hen

Once upon a time a little white hen ran away from the farmyard where she was born and set off for new adventure. She was tired of being cooped up in a narrow house all day with hens talking and clucking, and no green fields in which to walk. There was a wide world near her, and so she packed her nightdress and brush and comb, and escaped one fine day.

She walked and flew across the fields until she came to a warm yellow haystack built in a corner near a wall. 'I could make a house here,' said she to herself, and at once she dragged out some of the hay and built a small house. It had a roof of heavy grasses and a floor of beaten soil, and a window hole through which she could peep. There was a tiny trickle of water from a spring at the door and a round bowl of stone to drink from. Seeds were in the grasses of the haystack, and all was trim and neat.

She ate her supper and she got ready for bed. Then there was a tap at the door and a brown rabbit stood there.

'Is anyone here?' asked the rabbit.

'Oh, come in!' cried Mrs White Hen.

'I'm looking for lodgings,' said the rabbit. 'Have you any room to spare?'

'Oh yes,' said the hen. 'I shall be glad to have company, I have a spare room,' and she showed the rabbit a doorway into the haystack where another room was scooped out.

There was another tap, and a field-mouse looked in. 'Can you do with a helper?' she asked. 'I've helped many animals, and now I am free. I only want a few grains a day.' So the mouse came to live with the white hen and the brown rabbit.

The white hen was a good housekeeper. She swept the floor and brushed up the grains of wheat that the mouse brought in. She put them in a bowl ready to make bread. She made the little beds of scented hay and got fresh hay every week from the stack, just as human people put clean sheets on their beds. She washed the dishes and dried them with leaves. She polished the bits of furniture, a table and three stools, with beeswax which the bees gave her from their store. She made jam with wild raspberries and bilberries, and she mixed spring water with wild strawberries to make strawberry wine to drink.

'Dear Henny Penny,' said the brown rabbit. 'We do love you. You make such a cosy home for us.'

'Oh, indeed,' said the hen, ruffling her wings and making her eyes sparkle. 'Oh, I must say you do not help very much. You come in with dirty feet out of the mud, and forget to find the wheat ears. You don't help me enough.'

The rabbit bowed his head. It was true. He liked to leap and run and play games, he liked to peep at the sky, and to nibble parsley in a garden, or steal a green lettuce from the farmer, or dodge away from the farmer's dog.

He had no cares in the world, and he ran out of the little hay house and left the good white hen to carry on with the help of the tiny mouse.

The mouse scuttered in and out, carrying grains of corn, finding juicy morsels to eat, filling the kettle with water from the spring, helping to hang out the clothes on washday, but she was so little she could not do very much.

One fine day the big red fox who lived in the rocky wood came down the hill to the cornfield. He was hungry after the long winter, and he began to hunt for food.

Then he saw something white, and it was the little white hen coming from her house of hay.

'I've never seen any hens there before,' said the fox to himself. 'I could do with a nice little hen, and white hens are the tastiest. I'm in luck today.'

He crept slowly down, hiding in the cover of long grass, till he came near the hen's house. Then he lay flat and waited. He could hear the

hen singing in the house, and this is what she
sang:

Oh, little white hen,
Lend me a pen,
And I will write a story.
The rabbit and mouse
They leave the house,
And you work there in your glory.

A weed tickled the fox's nose and he sneezed. The
hen stopped her song and listened. 'A-tishoo,'
sneezed the fox again.

'Oh dear,' said the little white hen. 'Somebody's got a cold. Where's the blackcurrant tea?
Poor thing.'

She poured out a cup of hot blackcurrant tea
and took it to the door. There lay the fox, and she
trembled so much she spilled the tea.

'Oh! Oh!' she cried, turning back, but the fox
put out a paw and waved it gently in the air.

'Oh, I'm dying. I'm dying,' he murmured
feebly, and he shut his eyes and moaned.

'Poor thing,' said the hen, and she poured the
rest of the blackcurrant tea into his open mouth.
The fox licked his lips, it was delicious, and he
changed his mind in that moment. He decided he
would not eat the little white hen. He had a better
plan.

'Little White Hen,' he cried in a faint voice.
'You have saved my life. Will you honour me by

coming to my home, and being my housekeeper? Beautiful White Hen, please come and help a timid fox.'

The white hen fluttered her wings and stilled her panting heart, and the fox smiled a crooked smile and lured her on. He had a magical way with him.

'Beautiful Hen,' said he, 'come back with me and help an old bachelor fox to manage his untidy house. I can see at a glance you are a good house-keeper.'

The hen smiled at this. 'Sir, I accept your offer,' said she, making a curtsey, and the fox bowed his head.

'Wait a few minutes while I fill my bag and get ready,' said she.

She went back to the house, filled her little bag with a nightdress and brush, and a spare scarf for her neck. Then out she tripped.

The fox was waiting. 'She's very skinny,' said he to himself. 'I can wait a few weeks.'

'You have been working too hard, little hen,' said he to her. 'You need a holiday and I will take care of you.'

'Thank you, sir,' said the hen. 'Yes, the brown rabbit does not help me very much. He is too young and foolish.'

'The brown rabbit?' echoed the fox. 'I have not met him yet.'

'No, sir. He is out playing in the fields,' said the

innocent hen.

She followed the fox across the fields, up the pasture into the woods. They came to a big black stone. 'My front door,' said the fox. He lifted a curtain of brambles and the hen hesitated. 'After you, dear White Hen,' said he politely, and he followed the hen into the house.

It was rather dark, but the fox drew back the window curtain and there was a view down the valley. Far away the hen could see the top of the haystack, but her little home was hidden in the hollow.

'Shall I make a cup of tea?' she asked, and the fox said he would be delighted. There was a little fire smouldering in the grate and he blew it into flames with a blow-bellows.

'That's a fine windy thing, sir,' said she admiringly. 'I've never seen one before.'

'It's to save your breath, Mrs Hen,' said the fox.

He filled the kettle for her and she made the tea, using a pinch of herbs from a canister on a shelf.

'Dear me,' said she, 'your house is rather dusty,' and she picked up a duster and wiped the table and a chair. Big cobwebs hung from the ceiling, but the fox said he liked a cobweb, and a spider was company for a lonely fox.

'Baked spider makes a nice supper,' said the hen.

'Yes,' replied the fox dreamily. 'But I will go to

market, and you shall have better food than baked spider, Mrs Hen. You are rather thin, my dear. You need some good food.'

The hen smiled and at once went about her work. There was a lot to do, but she soon had a clean house for the fox.

So the days passed, and the little white hen looked after the fox, and gave him many a comfort. But he had to wipe his feet and to eat his meals in a secret rocky dell lest he alarm his little housekeeper.

One day the white hen noticed a pheasant's feather on the hearth, and a guinea-fowl's tail in the garden. She was worried over this for she thought the fox was a good vegetarian.

He stayed out late at night, and locked the door so that she could never go into a field alone.

'It isn't safe, little Hen,' he told her. 'A wolf hunts at night. He would eat you.'

'A wolf!' she cried, her eyes wide with fright. 'No, I won't go out alone, sir.'

The fox often sat reading a green book which he kept on a shelf in the house. Once when he was out Mrs Hen flew up to the shelf and turned the pages. She was horrified at the tales she read.

'How to lure a pheasant off a tree' was one story, and another was called 'How to catch a duck swimming', and 'How to catch a sleeping rabbit'.

She turned the pages, and found the way to lure a hen from its nest, by flattery and praise.

At the end of the book two pages were stuck together, and she pressed her sharp beak between them and read the tale.

'A charm against an enemy: cowslips are the flowers of magic,' she read. 'Weave a garland of cowslip flowers, freshly gathered, and put it around your neck. No harm shall follow, for you shall be rendered invisible to your foe. This is a certain cure for all terrors.'

She pressed the leaves together again and flew down to the floor to ponder what she had read.

'I am in danger,' she thought. 'I am here in a fox's den, and at any time he might eat me. I must try that magical cure, if only I can get some cowslips.'

So she went carefully about her duties, and the fox continued to smile at her, but she noticed a sharp look he gave her at times.

All this time the brown rabbit and the little mouse had been trying to manage alone. They missed the little hen and her charming company. They had nobody to tell them a story or to make the beds and cook the meals.

'Where can she be?' they asked one another.

'Perhaps she flew away because I did not help her,' confessed the brown rabbit.

'I don't think she would leave us, for she loved us,' said the mouse, consoling the rabbit.

'I shall go and look for her in the hills,' said the rabbit.

'Please take care,' begged the mouse.

So in the evening as the sun was setting, the brown rabbit set off to look for the white hen. He trotted in hollows and ditches, he visited farms and cottages, and although he saw many a hen none was as pretty and neat as his friend.

'I've heard there's a white hen imprisoned in the fox's lair, up in the rocks,' whispered a hedge-hog. 'He says she's his housekeeper, he boasts about her, but I cannot believe she stays there for fun. Besides, I've never seen her going for walks.'

The rabbit nodded his head, and asked the way, and the hedgehog described the house among the rocks in the wild wood.

Soon the rabbit reached the house, and he had no doubt about it for he could hear the hen singing a song to herself. He tapped at the window and the song stopped. The hen came running to look out and when she saw the rabbit she rushed to the door and invited him in.

'Oh, my darling Rabbit,' she cried, throwing her wings around him. 'Here I am in the fox's house, and you must not stay or he might eat you. He is out now, but any minute he may return.'

'But why . . . what . . . what are you doing?' asked the rabbit.

'I'm the fox's housekeeper, but I think, I think he will eat me some day,' sighed the hen. Then she added, 'But you can save me. Yes, please pick a bunch of cowslips from Cowslip Field and bring them here tomorrow night. I can escape, I think. Oh, Rabbit, do help me!'

'Of course I will, Henny Penny. I will come when the moon peeps over the hill. If the fox is here I will put the cowslips under the window for you.'

'If he is not in the house I will put a glow-worm on the windowsill, and you can come in, but if he is indoors it will be darkness, and you must hurry off,' said the hen.

So off ran the rabbit, joyfully, and although the fox passed him on the way they did not see each other.

The next day the rabbit went to the field called 'Cowslip Field', and he picked a bunch of the sweet flowers. Then when the moon was rising behind the hill he ran to the house in the wood. On the windowsill glowed a green glow-worm, and the rabbit tapped at the door boldly.

'Oh, thank you, Rabbit,' cried the hen. 'I will make the magical wreath, and you must hurry home to tell the mouse I am coming. Good-bye, and be quick before the fox comes.'

Away ran the rabbit like a shadow in the dusk, and the white hen began at once to make the wreath. She threaded the cowslips into one another, by piercing the stalks with her beak and slipping the next stalk through each split flower-stalk. The cowslips were large, with many bells, and the wreath was very beautiful. When she had used all the flowers, she slipped the wreath over her head and then went to a broken piece of glass in which the fox used to admire himself. She saw nobody, and this gave her a shock for a moment, until she realized that she was invisible to everyone, including herself. She heard a step and in came the fox.

'White Hen! White Hen!' he called, and the hen stood still, scarcely breathing.

'White Hen! Where are you hiding?' called the fox. He ran upstairs and down, into kitchen and outhouse and garden. He could not find the invisible hen, but the hen did not wait any longer. She stepped boldly out while he was in the garden, and away she went down the path through the wood, past the masses of dark rocks, past the ferns and primrose glades, away she went. Sometimes she flew a few yards, but she was afraid the cowslips might slip. So she ran.

At last she came to her old home beside the haystack, and she pushed open the door. The mouse and the rabbit sat talking, and when the door opened they stared, for nobody came in.

The hen danced round the room chuckling and crowing. Then she took the cowslip wreath from around her neck.

'I'm visible now,' said she. 'Did you ever know such magic? My dear Rabbit and little Mouse, I've come home to you.'

'I'll get the supper,' said the rabbit quickly,

and he brought a fine lettuce and some corn in a dish to the table.

After supper they all tried on the wreath of cowslips. The mouse was invisible because she was completely hidden by the flower, but the rabbit danced and leapt with the wreath bobbing on his shoulders, and they tried to catch him by following his voice.

Then the hen told her adventures, how she had been lured away by the fox, and treated kindly, but she was not sure – no, not sure of what might happen. She was so glad to come home to freedom and fun with her friends, she said.

She hung the wreath on the wall and there it may be seen to this day, for it never faded away or lost its scent.

When the white hen wishes to be invisible she wears the garland and tricks everyone, even the rabbit. When it is the rabbit's turn to wear the garland, he can hide from the white hen. As for the mouse, she is invisible without any cowslips, for she digs a hole and hides.

The fox missed the little white hen, but one day he met a beautiful vixen, and he married her and they lived in the dark house among the rocks where a family of little foxes was born. The father fox told the story of the white hen who disappeared and all the little foxes stared at him. They hoped they would find the little white hen, and that she would tell them stories.

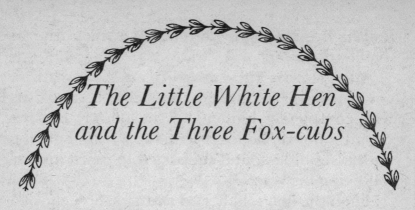

The Little White Hen and the Three Fox-cubs

The little white hen clucked happily as she dusted her house, under the shadow of the new haystack. There was a sweet scent in the air, the smell of haymaking, of meadow-sweet, creamy flowers in the ditch by the hedge, of honeysuckle waving its crowns over the bushes.

'I wish we could keep these nice smells all the year,' she thought, and she ran out of doors to look at the sun.

The brown rabbit hopped up to her, and pulled her tail feathers.

'What are you sniffing about, dear White Hen?' he asked.

'Sweet smells,' replied the hen. 'But don't pull my tail, Rabbit, or I shall pull yours.'

'You can't. It's too small,' chuckled the rabbit, and he leapt in the air and caught a butterfly and let it go.

'I went to sea and caught a whale,
I held it by its fishy tail,'

sang the rabbit.

'Silly young rabbit,' muttered the hen, and she went to the bed of meadow-sweet and collected some flower heads like white tassels.

'What are you doing, White Hen?' asked the rabbit.

'I'm going to make scent, to remind us of summer when winter comes,' she replied

'I can remember,' laughed the rabbit, but he thought it was a good plan.

They ran through the field nipping a flower now and then, a spray of honeysuckle, which the hen flew up to gather, a few heads of clover, some purple wild thyme from the hot bank, and some wild roses which hung down close to the ground.

Soon they had enough to fill a basket, and the hen carried them back to the house with the rabbit dancing behind her. The little mouse was looking everywhere for her friends.

'Oh White Hen, I couldn't find you. Why have you picked all those flowers? Are they for supper?' she asked.

'They are to make scent,' said the hen. 'To make a nice smell in the house and all about us, when snow comes.'

The mouse looked startled. She had never heard of such a thing. Scents were in the haystack, and who could make them last?

But the white hen was determined. She asked the bees and butterflies to tell her of the sweetest flowers.

'Lavender,' said the bees.

'Lavender?' cried the hen. 'I don't know about it.'

'It grows only in gardens,' said the bees. 'But in far countries it is wild. Our fields are too cold for it, so it grows in warm gardens.'

'Then we will go to the gardens and pick it,' said the hen, nodding her head.

At dusk she flew across the fields to the garden of the farm by the common. She slipped through a gap in the hedge and walked softly down a paved path.

A puppy met her and gave a bark, but the hen was not frightened.

'Please, little dog, can you tell me where I can find a flower called lavender?' she asked.

'Lavender?' cried the astonished dog. 'Why, this hedge is made of lavender. My mistress uses it for sweet smells.'

'Please, may I have some?' asked the hen, humbly, and the dog said she might.

She nipped off many heads of the purple flowers, and the dog helped her. Soon she had a sheaf of lavender, and she tucked it under her arm.

'Will you accept this gift for your mistress?' she asked the dog. She held out a white feather, smooth as silk, shining like silver.

'Thank you, little White Hen,' said the dog. 'I will give it her.'

'It is a pen,' said the white hen. 'I have put a

point on it and your mistress can write with it.'

'She is only a little girl,' said the dog. 'She doesn't write very much, but she will like it.'

Then away went the hen and the dog rushed into the farmhouse to find the little girl.

'What have you got there, Dusky?' asked the child.

'A pen,' barked the dog. 'It came from a white hen.'

'It's a feather pen,' cried the girl, 'and I do believe it came from the white hen who lives by the old stack in the field. She is my favourite hen. I'm sure it is a magical pen,' she cried in delight.

'Little White Hen, little White Hen,
She sends you a snowy feathery pen,
The pen won't write for gentlemen,
Who never can find the little White Hen,'

wrote the pen in delicate flowing writing on the paper, and the little girl took the letter to her father.

'It's that white hen as lives by our haystack,' said he. 'We must not disturb her or she will fly away. She brings us luck, my little Lucy.'

But the hen took home the sheaf of lavender and the mouse stripped the fragrant heads from the long stalks, and the hen put them into a fine lawn handkerchief she once found on the common. She filled the handkerchief bag and sewed it up with little stitches, using a thorn for a

51

needle and the fine stalks of the stitchwort flower for cotton.

Then the three friends spread out the other flowers, the honeysuckle, the wild thyme, the bed-straw, the clover and the water mint, to dry on a stone slab in the hot sun. All day the flower heads dried, but at night the hen covered them up with hay to keep them from the dew.

In a few days the flowers were dry, but their smell remained. The rabbit sniffed at them, the mouse rubbed her nose among them and the white hen took up a few flowers and tossed them in the air to show how light they were. They all smelled very sweet but the lavender was the best of all, so the hen fetched more and more lavender from the garden.

She sewed small bags from some foxglove leaves, using a horse-hair to sew them in tiny stitches. Then she filled the bags with the dried flower heads, and put them about the house where they shed their sweet odour.

Now, across the valley and near the top of the hill, lived Mr Fox and his three little cubs and his wife. The fox remembered the little white hen who had once been his housekeeper, and he often talked about her to his sons.

'The white hen used to tell me stories,' said he. 'She told me about Jack the Giant-killer, and Cinderella, and Puss-in-Boots, and about the fox who wore magical shoes which ran as fast as the wind.'

'Oh, do tell us,' said the little foxes.

'Well, once on a time there was a little fox called Cinderella,' began the fox, 'and she lived in an untidy kitchen. Her two sisters would not do any work.'

The little foxes laughed and cuddled closely together.

'Like us,' they chuckled.

'Then one day they went to a dance in the barn where the King of the Foxes lived, but Cinderella was left at home.'

'Poor Cinder,' cried the little foxes. 'What next?'

'I want my dinner,' yawned the father fox. 'I could eat a little white hen. Just go off and find her, children.'

So off the little foxes went to find the white hen.

She was sitting in the sun making lavender-bags when they came galloping, rolling and skipping down the hill.

'Three little foxes,' said the white hen, calmly, but her heart fluttered and her wings trembled.

'You go home, little rabbit and mouse. I will meet the foe,' said she.

So the mouse and the rabbit scuttered into the shelter of the house, under the shade of the hay-stack, and the white hen waited.

'Hello,' cried the fox-cubs, stopping near her and staring at her snowy feathers. Her yellow eyes sparkled, and she nodded her head and went on sewing.

'Can you tell us about Cinderella?' asked the three foxes.

The hen chuckled, but she went on sewing.

'Come closer,' she urged. 'I won't eat you.'

They gasped, for her beak was sharp and they were rather scared. They crept nearer and the sweet smell of the lavender came to them in waves.

'Well,' said Mrs White Hen. 'Well, Cinderella had no carriage to go to the ball, but a little white hen came from the farmyard and it tapped on a stone and a carriage came out of it. Four rats came up and opened the carriage door for Cinderella, and another rat took the reins, and two little foxes pulled the carriage. Off they went to the ball.'

She stopped a minute and the little foxes nearly burst their skins with delight. 'What then?' they asked.

'Well, she wore four shoes of lavender, like these flowers, and she danced so lightly and sweetly that the Prince of the Foxes fell in love with her.'

'Oh! Oh!' cried the foxes, and each felt he was a prince.

'Well!' said the hen, eyeing them. 'The church

clock struck twelve, and everything disappeared, and the little fox scampered home in three lavender shoes, losing one on the way. And she sat on the hearth so that nobody knew she had ever gone away.'

'What next?' asked the little foxes.

'The Prince found one of the lavender shoes in the farmyard, and he tried to find the other shoes. He hunted up and down the hills until he came to the fox's den and there, drying in the sun, were three lavender shoes. He brought the other one from his pocket and entered.

' "Does Cinderella live here?" he asked.

"Yes," said the little fox.

"Is this her shoe?" he asked.

"Yes, sir," said Cinderella.

"I want to marry her. Bring your shoes and come to the palace."

'So the little fox picked up the four shoes, put all four on her neat small feet, and skipped off to the palace in the barn. She was married to the Prince of the Foxes and she lived happily ever after.'

'Please make us some lavender shoes, little White Hen,' implored the excited foxes, so the hen quickly wove a dozen little shoes of lavender, while the foxes waited. Then, thanking her, they galloped home and their feet were so light they nearly flew.

'Oh Father! Oh Father!' they cried as they rushed into the house. 'Oh, Father!'

'Have you got the little white hen?' asked the fox crossly. 'You've been a long time catching her, and I'm hungry.'

'Oh, Father, she made us lavender shoes, and we can be Princes,' they cried, dancing up and down the floor.

Mr Fox was annoyed with his children, but when one of them stood in the middle and sang a song, his heart softened.

'Listen, Father. I know a song,' said the youngest little fox, and he sang:

'Once upon a time there were three little foxes,
All of them wore fine lavender sockses,
They kept them clean in foxglove boxes,
Did these three little, good little, clever young foxes.'

Mr Fox began to laugh, for he liked a song. He could never teach his sons to catch hens. Instead they danced at night in their lavender shoes, all across the hills, past the cottages and farms, even round the streets of the market town. Nobody could catch them when they wore lavender shoes, and the dogs never chased them, for the smell of lavender went with them instead of the foxy smell the dogs knew.

As for the little white hen, she was never afraid of the fox-cubs, and she told them more tales when they came to visit her, tales of Sleeping Beauty, and Puss-in-Boots and Red Riding Hood, and the three little foxes always sat quietly listening under the light of the stars, while the owls hooted and the ghosts waved their wings, listening too.

Then back home went the little foxes, saying, 'We do love the little white hen,' as they put their shoes in their boxes and went back to bed.

The Grey Stone

One fine day in winter, when the snow had forgotten to fall, and the wind had fallen asleep in the bare woods, eight little boys and a girl ran along a lane on their way home from school.

The little boys carried canvas dinner bags on their backs, but the little girl, who wore a red velvet cap, carried a basket. They trotted along, all talking at once, kicking the stones with their iron-tipped boots. The little girl had kicked a grey stone all the way from the village, where she had found it near the school gate, and now she was so intent on taking it home that she lagged behind the others.

'I'm going to have rabbit pie tonight,' said one boy, 'because my father killed a rabbit yesterday.'

'I'm going to have a bantam egg,' cried another. 'Our bantam laid a tiddley egg this morning, and my muvver is boiling it for my tea.'

'I'm going to have chitterlings,' cried a third.

Then they all shouted what they were going to have, but some didn't know, so they just invented.

59

'I 'specks I'll have a gingerbread man with two currant eyes,' said a romantic little boy.

'What are you having, Amanda?' they called to the girl, who was busy following her stone across the road.

'I'm going to have Mimsey-cake!' she said proudly.

When they came to a group of cottages they separated, the boys running shouting through their wicket gates, banging at the doors, calling across the red-tiled floors to their mother. The little girl went farther on, still kicking the stone, until she, too, came to a small cottage set back from the road in a garden. She dribbled her stone up the path to the door, and then went in to have her Mimsey-cake.

The stone lay by the boot-scraper and stared about. This was the greatest luck! For years without end it had lain in the roads, kicked hither and thither by careless feet, ever since it had been quarried out of the great frowning cliff, and broken up by the roadman.

It had hoped to go to school, but, although it had been up and down the village street and into the lanes, it had never been as close to a door as this.

Always it had wanted to see the inside of a house, where those merry little feet lived, but the doors were closed. It had envied its brothers built into walls, but of course they had lost their freedom.

The door was flung open, but a rough little wind, which came curling down the valley, banged it to again.

'Prop the door open, Amanda,' cried a voice, and Amanda stepped outside.

She picked up the stone and put it inside the cottage, leaning against the door. The stone was actually inside the house! 'This is real life!' it thought.

It pushed hard and kept the door open, whilst Amanda's mother went out with a clothes basket, and returned with a pile of little garments. Then someone closed the door, and it was safe inside!

It squatted unnoticed in a corner, listening to the chatter, watching the baby in the cradle, and the cat and dog on the hearth. Nothing escaped the stone, and it enjoyed everything, from the familiar feel of Amanda's boots, which were kicked off and flung on top of it, to the scorch of hot tea, which the brimming teapot spilled over it.

When all the household had gone to bed, and the lamp was put out, and the fire damped down, the stone listened to the voices talking, the voices which were silent in the daytime, but audible in the quiet of night.

Mice ran over it, crickets leapt upon it, the grandfather clock ticked out a long history of things it had seen, the table grunted, the chairs squeaked, the canary awoke and peeped down through the bars of his cage at the stranger.

'They'll turn you out,' cried the clock, 'and you haven't heard half my story.'

'But I don't want to go,' replied the stone. 'I've been waiting for this for thousands of years, and I want a little comfort in my old age.'

'They'll throw you out,' repeated the clock, grimly, and all the little voices echoed, 'Throw you out.'

'What shall I do?' asked the stone, anxiously.

'Suppose you disguise yourself,' suggested the big arm-chair, and all the voices said, 'Disguise yourself.'

So the mice dragged Amanda's velvet cap, which lay on a stool and pulled it over the top of the stone, and the two boots moved in front of it, and a scarf fell down from behind the door and wrapped itself round its middle.

'What am I like?' asked the stone in a muffled tone, for it was smothered with clothes.

'Like Amanda,' cried everything at once. So the stone sat still with the cap on its head, and the scarf round its body, and the two boots with their iron tips in front, and it hoped it would be taken for Amanda.

'This is adventure!' it muttered, and rejoiced it had left the road.

But when Amanda came down in the morning she hunted for her boots to clean, and there they were beside her cap and scarf!

'Who threw my cap and scarf down there?' she demanded, as she kicked the stone under the sofa. But the clock ticked solemnly on, and the fire flickered, and her mother said, 'You must have done it yourself, Amanda, you are so very careless.'

All day the stone hid, and at night it joined the family party. Again the clock warned it of its fate.

'They'll throw you out,' it said.

Sure enough the next morning a sweeping

brush dragged it into the light.

'What's that stone doing there?' asked Amanda's mother as it rolled over towards the fire.

'It's the door-stop,' exclaimed Amanda.

How proud the stone felt, for it was the first time it had ever had a title!

Amanda's father stooped down and picked it up. He held it as if he would fling it through the open door, into the road beyond the garden.

The clock ticked, 'Good-bye, good-bye,' the chairs creaked, and a little mouse behind the wainscot gave a cry, which the cat heard, for she sprang up and walked towards the wall.

Then he changed his mind. He examined the stone carefully, first on one side, and then on the other. He fetched a hammer and gave it a tap.

Horrors! A piece flew off, and the pale stone turned even paler. Was it going to be made into dust?

He chipped off another piece.

'Whatever are you doing, Father?' asked his wife, and Amanda stared up at him.

'See here,' he cried. 'Yon's a fossil.'

Inside the stone was a group of dark ferns, perfect in their exquisite grace, their tiny fronds as clear as if they had been pressed in the stone that day.

'The place for this is on the chimney-piece,' he continued, impressively. 'I thought there was something in this bit of stone as soon as I saw it. It's the best fossil I've ever found in all my born days, and I'm a quarryman and ought to know.'

So they placed it on the mantelpiece along with a shell in which the sea roared, and two china dogs with chains round their necks.

Every time a visitor came it was taken down and displayed in all its beauty. Every day it listened to the children's talk, as they came in from school to look at Amanda's fossil. But every night it listened to the secret voices which wove romantic stories out of the mists of past ages.

The Fairy in a Cage

One day Dick Trelawney found a fairy! You don't believe it? It is true, nevertheless, and I will tell you how it came about.

Dick's mother was busy washing blankets, the big fluffy blankets with red borders off her own bed, and the little fluffy ones with blue borders off Dick's bed. She was so busy that when Dick asked if he might have a jam turnover, she said, 'Yes, don't bother me, child;' and when he asked if he might have an apple from the old tree in the garden, she said, 'Yes,' although it would give him a pain; and when he asked if he might go into the Wild Wood, she said 'Yes,' although she had never let him go there alone before.

So off Dick ran, with the jam turnover in one hand, and the apple in the other. He climbed the high fence, and ran into the wood among the beech and nut trees, the oak trees, and the silver birches. At first it was fun, for squirrels shouted to one another, 'Here's Dick Trelawney, coming into our wood,' and Dick threw fir cones to them to see if they would catch them.

Rabbits sat up on their hind legs, rubbing their paws together in amazement as they saw Dick's brown legs twinkling through the leaves, and his blue eyes sparkling. They didn't run away, they just sat and watched him, and Dick threw them a morsel of turnover, which they ate with dainty nibbles.

It was all very exciting, and when Dick had stirred up an ants' nest, and seen a green wood-pecker climb a tree, and a sleepy owl hide in an ivy-covered oak, his joy was complete. He whistled and sang, walking along with his hands in his pockets and his head thrown back to see the wonders of Wild Wood.

Would he meet a blue Dragon, or see a Unicorn fight a Lion, or get a view of a Witch sitting at the door of her little butterscotch house, waiting to invite him in? He wouldn't go. Not he! He knew better than that, and he whistled louder than ever.

But the wood grew denser, and the trees crowded together. Holly trees pricked him, and ropes of ivy tried to trip him. Brambles lay across his path, with thorns which tore his clothes. It was dark, too, for the branches kept out the sun-light, but Dick stumbled along, worming his way through the gaps, clutched at by twigs like fingers, grabbed by little pointed leafy hands. The rabbits had gone, and only the scream of the jay could be heard, high up in the top boughs.

'Go away, go away,' it seemed to cry, and Dick tried to turn round, but could not. In front he saw a glimmer of light, and at last he struggled into a patch of sunshine. It was a circle of mossy ground, starred with golden flowers, with club moss, with scarlet toadstools, and yellow pimpernel. The sun blazed down on the open space where butterflies hovered and sipped of the flowers.

In the middle lay something, a big moth, or a tiny bright bird, fast asleep. Even as he stooped to look at the delicate wings, it awoke and stretched itself. Then Dick saw it was a fairy.

Quick as lightning he darted his fingers down on the winged creature and caught her. She fluttered in his hands, and beat against his flesh, kicking and biting, so he popped her in his handkerchief, tied the corners, and started off home.

Strange to say, the trees parted for him, and the way was easy.

'Let me out, let me out,' cried a shrill voice, thin as a grasshopper's, but Dick only laughed. He meant to keep his fairy.

The rabbits and squirrels knew what he had caught, for they came close to him with their noses against his bare legs, so that he could have caught them too, if he had wished. He even stroked one small rabbit, which sat at his feet with paws uplifted, as if to beg him to let the fairy go.

They followed him till he came to the fence, and then they ran back to the wood.

Dick Trelawney ran home to the orchard where his mother was pegging out the blankets in the sunshine.

'I've caught a fairy, Mother,' he cried.

'Nonsense, child, no one ever caught a fairy,' said she. 'It's a butterfly.'

'No, it's a fairy. I'm going to keep it in our bird-cage, and watch it fly,' said Dick, 'and I shan't let it get away, ever.'

He ran indoors, and went to the lumber room, where an old bird-cage lay among the boxes and trunks. He opened the handkerchief and toppled the fairy inside.

She stood with ruffled hair and crumpled wings, a frown on her elfin face, and her little fists tightly clenched. She stamped and hissed at him, and he saw her green eyes flash. Then she flew to a perch and cried a little, so that her tears rolled down on the floor of the cage.

She buried her small pointed face in her two hands, and bowed her tiny shoulders as she drooped. Dick had not expected this. He thought fairies were always happy, and he ran off for a lump of sugar, which he thrust between the bars. But the fairy pushed it away, and sprang into a corner.

All day she moped, although Dick stroked her

with a feather, and poured rose leaves in the cage. She would not move, she would not speak, or fly, or sing.

At night the fairy, who crouched like a sad green bird in the corner of the cage, was covered by a cloth, and the Trelawneys went to bed.

Then strange things began to happen.

The house door flew open, and a cold wind came bustling in. The blankets, airing round the half-dead fire, flopped off the clothes-horse, and ambled into the garden, where they lay down to sleep on the earth under the gooseberry bushes. The clothes-horse itself frisked round the kitchen.

and then galloped down the garden path to the gate, which it straddled.

'What's that noise?' asked Mrs Trelawney, sitting up in bed, but her husband only snored, and she lay down again.

But the fairy snatched the cloth off the cage, and stared about with a glittering eye. The china mugs climbed down from the dresser, the teapot scrambled from the shelf, the fire-irons gathered themselves together, and off they all went, with a clatter and rattle and crash as they bumped each other.

'Mercy-on-us,' cried Mrs Trelawney, shaking her husband. 'There's burglars or bewitchery downstairs.'

They sprang out of bed and came running downstairs in their nightgowns. The arm-chair was racing along on its castors, followed by a prancing rocking chair, and a jigging three-legged stool.

'Stop, stop,' they cried, throwing themselves on the furniture, but nothing could hinder the flight, and out they went, dragging Mr and Mrs Trelawney with them as if they were feathers. The strength of the things! Even the footstool and the warming-pan danced out, and hurled themselves across the garden, till they fell over the cabbages and beans!

The room was empty now, except for the bird-cage, which swung to and fro, with the fairy.

Suddenly she began to laugh and laugh, and the sound was like a tinkle of silver, hard and sweet, beautiful and cruel.

Mr Trewlawney lighted a lantern, and Mrs Trelawney put a coat over her nightgown. They covered the cage with a tablecloth, and then searched for their belongings. They lifted the un-resisting chairs and stool back again, and tidied up as best they could. Then they went to bed, tired and cross.

'It's that fairy up to her tricks,' said Mrs Trelawney to Dick. 'I've heard of their goings on when they are bound to mortals. You must let her go tomorrow.'

'Yes, take her back to the wood, and see she doesn't come here again,' said Mr Trelawney, as he heaved himself into bed and blew out the candle.

When Dick looked at the fairy the next morn-ing, she flew to the swing at the top of the cage, spreading her bright wings to catch the light. She swayed to and fro, singing in a tiny voice like a distant nightingale, exquisite, low, so soft it could scarcely be heard, yet so full of sadness it hurt Dick's heart.

'I shall have to let her go today,' he cried, 'but how I wish I could keep her! Perhaps if I put her in the apple tree she couldn't do any harm.'

'No, no, no,' trilled the fairy, looking more and

more like a green bird, but her eyes were wild and·
dangerous.

At breakfast the table rocked, and the stool
trotted towards the door. The loaf of bread
danced on the table, and the cups began to move.

Dick's father sprang up with a roar.

'Be off at once with that fairy, Dick. I can't get
my breakfast.'

Dick lifted the cage from the hook and put on
his cap. The fairy sang softly, beating her wings,
and swinging up and down. Her silky hair floated
behind her, and her green eyes mocked the per-
turbed little household.

'Hurry up, Dick,' cried Mrs Trelawney, as a
rumbling came from the bedroom. 'There's something a-doing upstairs.' A jug and basin rolled
down the stairs, and came prancing across the
room.

Dick ran off, carrying the cage at arm's-length.
The trees and flowers bowed as if the wind were
passing, although the air was still.

Louder sang the fairy, and the robins and
thrushes stayed their songs, and flew after the old
cage with the strange songster.

Away into the wood ran Dick, past the waiting
rabbits and field-mice, the squirrels and the voles,
which came from holes and nests to see a fairy in a
cage.

He ducked under swaying trees, and hurried by

the clinging bushes, till he came to the mossy spot where he had first found the little sprite. Then he opened the cage door and waited.

The fairy spread her wings and floated out like a film of gossamer. There was no sound, no beating of the air, no flutter of wings now. Silently she rose in the air, and her wings shone blue and green as the sunlight filtered through them, like beech leaves in Spring. Then she just faded away in the green of the trees.

Dick stared and stared, but she had gone. He sighed and picked up the cage. Then he trudged home, with never a song or a whistle.

But when Mrs Trelawney put away the cage that night she found many tiny pearls lying among the dead rose leaves. They were the fairy's tears. She gathered them up and sold them to a merchant in the big town, who gave her much gold for them.

But one she kept for Dick, and he has it yet, set in a ring, which he takes from a little leather box to show to his grandchildren, when he tells them this story.

The Rabbits go Hunting

Thomas Rabbit was pottering round his garden, looking at his vegetables all growing as fast as they could. There they were, rows of curly lettuces and crisp little radishes, and pink carrots with ferny leaves.

He smacked his lips as he thought of the feasts he would have with Maria, his wife, and with little Tim. But Tim had gone away for the whole day; it was very lonely without him. Thomas hoped the lettuces would be ready when he returned.

'How splendid they look!' said he, as he stooped down and touched the leaves with his furry paw.

Then he sprang back in disgust.

'Slugs again!' he cried. 'Maria! Maria! Slugs are eating our lettuces.'

Yes, there were families of slugs – babies, mothers, and grandmothers, besides enormous fat great-grandmothers, all eating away at the juicy green leaves! They never stopped to talk to one another, they just went on eating.

Maria came running up the long passage from the house underground, wiping the soap-suds from her paws.

'Oh! Thomas,' she cried, 'you must set some traps, some slug traps, and catch them all.'

So together they twisted fine grasses, and wove them into little traps, and weighted them with stones, and baited them with radishes. Such neat little trim little traps were never seen! Then they placed them round the garden.

But did the slugs walk in? Oh no! They laughed in the slimy way they have, and went on devouring the juicy lettuces.

'Deary me! What shall we do? There will be no lettuce left when little Tim comes home,' cried Maria, and she walked sadly back into the house with Thomas dejectedly following her.

They sat down to think, and then Thomas had a bright idea.

'I'll shoot the varmints,' said he, valiantly.

He reached for his little pop-gun which hung on the ceiling, took down his bag of peas, and pulled his shooting-boots over his furry feet.

'Good-bye, dear,' said he, kissing Maria.

''But you are only going to the garden, aren't you?' asked Maria, anxiously.

'Yes, but it's dangerous work, shooting slugs.'

'Good-bye, good-bye,' he called as he stepped bravely out into the open.

He crept warily up to a lettuce, and fired.

POP! POP! POP! POP! POP! went the little gun.

But did the slugs mind? Oh no! They laughed more than ever in the slimy way they have, and settled down to eat up the peas before they returned to the lettuces.

'How are you getting on?' whispered Maria, cautiously peering round the corner, when the sound of the pop-gun ceased, and all the peas had gone.

'It's no good, my dear,' sighed Thomas. 'We shall *never* have any lettuces left when little Tim comes home.'

They walked sadly down into the kitchen, and sat on the floor.

They thought and they thought, and then Maria had an idea.

'We must *frighten* them away,' said she. 'We'll play on squeaker grasses, and terrify those slugs.'

They ran out into the meadows and picked the long broad grasses. Then they both held one tightly across their front teeth, stooped over the lettuces and blew!

Such squeaks and squawks came from the little mouth-organs, such shrill and ugly sounds, that the birds looked down from the cherry trees in amazement, and then flew away.

The slugs raised their heads to listen.

'Music, sweet music at the feast!' they murmured to one another, and they waved their fat bodies joyously. They laughed happily in the slimy way they have, and went on devouring the lettuce.

Poor Thomas and Maria retired to a corner, out of breath, and threw away their squeaker grasses.

'It isn't any use,' sighed Thomas, 'we shall not have a single lettuce left when little Tim comes home.'

They sat for a long time in silence, listening to the soft nibble, nibble of the slugs.

'Should we try to poison them?' whispered Maria.

They ran down to their kitchen again, to prepare a poison cake.

'It must be nice,' said Thomas, 'so that they will eat it, and we must put a pinch of poison in at the end.'

Maria made a delicious cake, with icing on the top, but just before she popped it in the oven, she dropped into the middle a pinch of DEADLY POISON from the poppy-seed box.

Thomas carried it up, all brown and sugary, and placed it by the lettuce-bed. Then he waited, with Maria by his side.

The slugs raised their noses and sniffed. Then they swarmed round, and before you could say 'Jack Robinson,' they had eaten it all up!

'Jolly good cake!' said they, wiping their

mouths, and returning to the lettuce-bed, all eager to get on with their work.

Maria began to cry, and Thomas had to comfort her.

'It's no good,' she sobbed. 'There won't be the tiniest scrap of lettuce left when little Tim comes home.'

'Let's drown them,' said Thomas fiercely, as he watched Maria's tears dropping on the ground. 'Could you cry enough to drown them, Maria?' he added.

'Oh no!' cried Maria. 'I daren't stand weeping over them, but we could get a bucket of water, couldn't we?'

So they carried water from the pond in lily-leaf buckets, and poured it over the slugs.

'Nice cold drink,' mumbled the slugs, as they drank it, and washed in it, and had a little swim to refresh themselves. Then they laughed in their slimy way, and returned hungrier than ever to the lettuce-bed.

'Alas! Alack!' moaned Maria. 'There won't be even a nibble when our little Tim comes home.'

'Hello! Hello!' cried a voice, and up rushed Tim, hopping and skipping, and turning somersaults as he came to his father and mother.

'I've brought a friend to supper. But what's the matter?' he added, as he saw his parents sitting in a pool on the grass, with broken buckets and squeakers, and the pop-gun lying by their side.

'The slugs are eating all the lettuce,' said Thomas, drooping his ears with sorrow.

'And we can't stop them,' added Maria.

'Is that all?' laughed Tim. 'Why, my friend, Thrush, has just been saying he hoped you would have meat for supper, but I told him we only had lettuces, we are vegetarians.'

A slim young thrush stepped daintily across the grass.

'Can I help you, sir?' he asked, politely.

He hopped to the lettuce-bed, and gobbled up the babies, mothers, grandmothers, and the great-grandmothers before they had time to take to their slimy heels.

Maria and Thomas stood by in wonder at his appetite.

'Ho! Ho! They laugh best that laugh last!' cried Thomas, as the slugs disappeared. 'A bird in the garden's worth two in the wood, so come and have supper with us whenever you like, Mr Thrush. You'll always be welcome, won't he, Maria?

'Now for our lettuces!' he continued jovially, turning to little Tim. 'All's well that ends well!'

The Doll's House

Jemima Mouse was dancing through a field one day, climbing the stalks of wild barley to taste the fruit, nibbling a mushroom in a hollow, biting a juicy leaf, sucking a blade of sweet-tasting grass, when something red attracted her attention. It was not a bunch of roses or a red poppy, but something else.

She was startled, she 'froze', that is she became so still she was like a brown stone. Only her bright eyes moved. Then, cautiously, she took a step or two closer, and she stopped. She sniffed and sniffed and a strange smell came to her. It was the smell of wood and paint, mixed with flowers.

On a bank in the grass, under the shade of a clump of foxglove leaves, stood a very small house. No house had been there before, and this was different from every house Jemima knew. It was not a mouse's house, or a toad's castle, or a mole's heap of soil hiding his fort, or a harvest mouse's round nest woven in the cornstalks. It was a real little house made of wood with four glass windows and a red roof, a chimney and a green front door. It was a house for a very small human.

'Who lives here?' wondered Jemima Mouse, but she dare not tap on the little brass knocker or open the wee door or peep in at a window.

Instead she dashed away to find her brother Jeremy Mouse. Jeremy was climbing a tree. It was only a hawthorn bush but he wanted to eat the juicy red berries which mice and children find so tempting. These 'haws' taste like bread and he called them 'Mouse-bread'.

He saw Jemima running across the grass, and he hid until she was near, when he leapt down to frighten her.

'Boo!' he shouted in a loud squeak as he dropped by her side.

'Oh Jeremy!' she panted. 'I have found a house. Come quickly and look at it.'

'A house?' echoed Jeremy. 'What kind of house? Some houses are dangerous, Jemima,' said he.

'Not this house. It is too little. It is a fairy house,' said Jemima, taking her brother's arm and holding the lively mouse.

They walked away, along the tiny field tracks made by mice and frogs and spiders, paths invisible to humans but clear to the small animals.

'It's a witch's house,' said Jeremy when he saw

the little red roof and the green door and glass windows.

'Nonsense,' said Jemima. 'It's a fairy house, where pretty fairies live. Let's go in.'

They waited and watched, but nothing stirred. So they tiptoed silently to the green door and tapped. Nobody came. Nobody stirred in the little house and a butterfly perched on the red roof and fanned her wings.

'Quite safe,' she murmured softly.

They pushed the door and it swung open, and they saw a little hall and a flight of wooden stairs.

'Let's both go in together,' they whispered, and they boldly walked in and the door shut behind them.

They ran up the narrow stairs and pushed open a door. It led to a nursery with some little toys. There was a wooden rocking-horse and a basket, and some boxes containing seeds. They tasted the seeds and liked them. They climbed on the rocking-horse and swayed to and fro. Then they looked at two little beds, side by side. Each had a white sheet and a coloured bedcover with a lace edge, and a find downy pillow.

'Oh,' sighed Jemima, 'nobody here and all for us. Oh Jeremy! What lovely beds!'

They sprang on the beds and lay for a minute curled up in happiness.

There was a dressing-table with a small mirror

and a hair-brush. Everything was very small and pretty and the two mice were delighted. They had never seen such luxury. Their own hair-brush was a teasel brush and their mirror a pool of water. Their bed was a sheep's wool bed, and their toys were sticks and acorns.

Jemima shook her head with delight and nestled among the little blankets. Jeremy followed her example.

'I'm tired, Jemima,' he murmured. Jemima kicked off her little red shoes, and Jeremy tossed his brown hat in a corner. Soon they were both fast asleep and dreaming of warm sunshine and flowers of many colours.

Now there came across the common and into the field a little girl named Cora with her mother.

'Can you remember where you left it?' asked Mrs Green, crossly. 'It was very careless of you, Cora, to go and lose your pretty doll's house, all new and fresh. A cow may have trampled on it and broken it.'

Cora gave a little sob and stared about her. 'I left it over there,' said she, pointing to the bank of flowers. 'I thought it would look nice among the violets and stitchwort.'

They walked on, and then the little girl gave a cry and ran forward.

'Oh, Mother! There it is! It's safe!' And she sprang up the bank, parted the leaves, and disclosed the little red-roofed house with the green door and nothing amiss.

'I am glad for your sake, Cora,' said her mother, and added softly, 'and for mine, too. I liked this little house.'

The child picked up the house and wiped off the dew and moisture. It looked perfectly all right. No damage was done and she tucked it under her arm and went back home with her mother. They put the doll's house on the kitchen table to dry and left it there.

The two little mice slept on. The jolting had not woken them. They slept happy and safe.

A cat leapt on the table and sniffed round the doll's house, but nothing happened, and it leapt down and mewed to the little girl, who stroked it and talked to it.

'It's only the doll's house, Tommy,' said Cora. 'There's nothing for you,' and she put the cat out in the garden.

Evening came and a bright light was turned on in the kitchen. There was a rattle of washing-up and cooking and affairs of kitchen work. Jeremy awoke and sat up. He whispered uneasily. The cat moved round the doll's house, mewing anxiously, and Jemima shivered as she heard the sound.

'Jemima! There's a noise. Where are we?'

The little mouse also looked about her and sat up in a fright. 'There's a tiger outside,' said she to Jeremy. 'Are we in Africa, Jeremy?'

'Keep quiet, Jemima,' whispered Jeremy. 'Keep silent and we shall be safe.'

So they crouched down and waited, and sure enough the room grew dark, the people left and the cat walked away.

They pushed open their little door and ventured out. They could see in the dark, and there was nothing to alarm them. On the table were crumbs of bread and cake, morsels of cheese and scraps of pastry. They ate these greedily, for they were very hungry.

Then Jemima saw something wonderful. Down on the floor in a corner of the room was a tiny house with walls of wire shining like silver, and a piece of cheese hanging from a hook.

'Look, Jeremy,' she said, 'a mouse's house with the door open and a piece of cheese.'

They both ran down the table legs and stared at the little wire house, shining and bright in the moonlight. Even as they gazed at it a fat brown mouse came out of a hole and pushed them aside.

'Keep away. That's my house,' said the house-mouse, crossly. 'You go back to the fields where you belong.'

They stood hesitating and they watched him enter through the wide open door. He seized the cheese in his sharp teeth, tugged and, oh, horrors! Down fell the door with a crash and he was shut inside. He dashed to the door but could not push it open. He called and cried, and Jeremy and Jemima were very sorry for him.

'Let me out! Let me out!' he called. 'Dear kind field-mice, let me out!'

'How can we open the door?' asked Jeremy.

'Press the lever down and the door will lift up,' said the house-mouse.

So they tugged at the wooden lever on the roof of the little house. They swung on the wooden bar, and pressed with all their might. Slowly the

90

door was lifted up and the house-mouse squeezed through the crack. They let go and the door fell, but the mouse was safe.

'Thank you, kind field-mice,' said the house-mouse. 'You have saved my life. Come and meet my wife and family,' he invited, but Jeremy and Jemima declined.

'We must go home,' they said. 'Our mother will be anxious. We have been away all day. Goodbye, House-Mouse.'

'Well, good-bye and thank you again, good kind mice,' said the house-mouse.

He showed them the way through a hole in the wall down a drainpipe into the garden. Then they ran away and after a long walk they reached home safely.

'Where have you been?' asked Mrs Mouse as she hugged her two children.

'We found a fairy house, Mother, and we went to sleep in lovely beds,' said Jemima.

'And when we awoke we were in Africa and a tiger was prowling around,' said Jeremy.

'And then we escaped and we were nearly caught in a silvery house,' said Jemima.

'And we saved a mouse from a trap,' added Jeremy.

'Then we came home,' said Jemima.

'What a chapter of adventures,' said Mrs Mouse. 'But where are your red shoes, Jemima, and where is your brown hat, Jeremy?'

'We left them in the fairy house,' said Jemima.

The next day little Cora opened her doll's house. In the bedroom was a pair of tiny red shoes, and a brown hat lay on the floor. The beds had been slept in, the blankets were muddy.

'Fairies have been in my house, Mother!' said Cora to her mother. 'They left their shoes and a hat behind.'

'Yes, indeed! They must be fairy clothes,' agreed Cora's mother, and she wondered about this all her life.

Slipper-Slopper

Mrs Rabbit went to market one fine day, and there she bought a pair of fine brown leather slippers for her son.

'He will be a gentleman, a real gentleman, in these splendid slippers,' she said to herself as she hurried home along the lanes to the little house on the common.

'Here's a pair of slippers for you, Tim,' said she, taking them out of her string bag, which bulged with peas and beans and lettuces. 'You can wear them tomorrow. Always wear a new thing on a new day, my son.'

Tim was delighted with their slipperiness and shininess. He gazed at them whilst he and his mother sat at tea, and he nursed them in his arms all evening. He took them to bed with him, and slept with them hanging on the bedpost.

The next morning he awoke early and put them on his little slim feet. Never had he seen such a slippery pair of shoes! His feet went sliding in and out as he walked carefully downstairs, holding on to the banister lest the slippers should slip downstairs without him. 'Slipper-slopper' they went, as they flapped on each wooden step.

'Do fasten your slippers, Tim,' cried Mrs Rabbit, looking up from the frying-pan in which she was cooking mushrooms and wild sorrel leaves — a tasty rabbit dish.

'They won't stay on, Mother. They are such slippery slippers,' answered Tim, giving them a hitch as they dropped off at the heels.

All day he went slipper-slopper, up and down the fields and across the common. The grass was bruised as he stumbled along, and stones got between his toes. He tumbled down and scrambled to his feet again with a very pink face. The field-mice stopped to look at him, and they laughed up their furry sleeves.

'Look at little Tim Rabbit!' they whispered. 'He thinks he is a fine gentleman, wearing big slippers like that! They are too large for him. All he can do is to go slipper-slopper over the meadows, like Emily Duck.'

Tim was much annoyed, but although he tied his fine slippers with twists of Hare Grass. and stuffed leaves in the toes, still they flipped and flopped as he walked.

So he sat down, and took them off, and hung them up in a gorse-bush! Then he pattered home without them.

Mrs Rabbit went to market again next week,

and returned with another pair of slippers for her son. 'He will be like a dainty maiden in these,' she said to herself, as she tripped along the path. 'There never has been such a pretty pair of slippers on our common within living memory.'

'Try these, Tim,' said she, taking them out of her little rush basket, along with apples and onions.

Tim looked with sparkling eyes at the little red slippers. He was sure they would not go slipper-slopper, they were so neat and trim.

He was happy at their brightness and redness, and he took them to bed with him, and slept with them under the pillow.

The next morning he came downstairs, wearing the pretty red slippers. 'Squeak! Squeak! Squeak!' they went.

'Don't make such a noise, Tim. I can't hear myself fry,' exclaimed Mrs Rabbit, looking up from the pan where the eggs sizzled.

'I can't help it, Mother. They won't be quiet,' said Tim, giving his slippers a tap of annoyance.

All day the little slippers squeaked, out of the burrow, into the wood, across the fields and spinney. 'Squeak!' they went, like a couple of mice.

The ants ran out of his way when they heard Tim coming, and the beetles scurried up the ferns to watch him pass. The squirrels sat in the trees, laughing at him behind their furry paws.

'Oh! Look at Tim Rabbit! He thinks he is a niminy-piminy lady, wearing slippers like that, and all he can do is to go Squeak! Squeak! like a flitter-mouse on a summer night!'

Tim was rather cross, and he wrapped cool dock-leaves round his slippers, but still they wouldn't be silent. He soaked them in the stream and rubbed them with dandelion juice, but they squeaked even louder. So he took them off, and hung them in a blackberry-bush. Then he ran pitter-patter home.

A week later, Mrs Rabbit went to market again, and on a stall kept by an ancient dame, she found a pair of remarkable slippers. She packed them with her gooseberries and carrots, and carried them home in triumph. 'A fairy might wear these slippers,' she told herself, as she walked through the fields.

'Try these slippers, Tim,' cried she gaily, and she took the tiny pair from her green-leaf parcel. 'These won't squeak or slipper-slopper. I paid a mighty price for them!'

Tim looked at the little white slippers, soft and dainty, and he laughed with glee. They were wonderful! He was sure they wouldn't go 'Squeak! Squeak!' or 'Slipper-slopper'.

He put them on the tablecloth and admired them all evening, and at night he carried them carefully upstairs, and slept with them cuddled to his heart.

The next day at cock-crow he was up, dancing round his room in the little slippers. Then he ran downstairs, and the little white slippers made no sound at all, not a breath or rustle.

'Oh! How you startled me!' cried Mrs Rabbit, jumping up and dropping the toast in the fire. 'How quiet you are, Tim!'

'They don't make any noise, Mother,' answered Tim, stooping down to stroke his little slippers.

He padded out of the house, over the fields, and on to the moor. The bumble-bees and the peacock butterflies didn't hear him coming, till he frightened them with his shadow. The blackbird jumped out of his way with a fluttering heart, and the thrush cried out in terror as he drifted by.

''Pon my word, Tim Rabbit! I thought you were a stoat,' he exclaimed. 'Why don't you walk properly? It isn't manners to startle your friends!'

The hedgehogs sat under the furze, laughing at him from behind their prickles.

'Look at Tim Rabbit!' they cried. 'He thinks he is a fairy, dancing away on those white slippers, and all the time he is only like a shadow, a nothing, a nothing-at-all. Ho! Ho!'

Tim was now very cross indeed, and he picked a peascod from the little wild pea, and popped it in his slippers to make a rattling noise, but the slippers were silent. He tried to sing, to shout, to whistle, but his voice was like the drifting leaves whilst he wore the magic slippers.

So he took them off, and hung them in a hawthorn-tree, where they looked like a bunch of May.

When he got home Mrs Rabbit exclaimed, 'Now, Tim! Here you are without any slippers again! I shan't get any more for you. You must go out tomorrow and find all the lost pairs, and then I can take them back to the market.'

So Tim sat quietly by the fire, and he wondered where his slippers were.

When he came down next morning, he skipped up to his mother on his little furry toes, and gave her a hug.

'Come along, Tim,' she laughed, and she poured the porridge into the little wooden bowls and put the honey on the table.

'It is nice to have no slippers. I don't want to be a fine gentleman, or a niminy-piminy lady, or even a fairy,' said he, and he rubbed his feet together under the table, and screwed up his happy toes. But he had not forgotten that he had to find all those lost slippers.

He ran to the gorse-bush, and the blackberry-bush, and the hawthorn-tree, but the slipper-slopper slippers, and the squeaking slippers, and the dainty fairy pair had all gone. He scampered up and down, in and out of burrows, in woods and fields and copses, seeking in hedges and ditches, in nooks and crannies. The other rabbits hunted

with him, but no one could find the lost slippers.

Where had they gone? The brown pair had been taken from the gorse-bush by little Jenny Wren. The red pair had been taken from the blackberry-bramble by Cock Robin. The white pair had been taken from the hawthorn-tree by Mr Magpie.

So Tim played hide-and-seek with all the other rabbits, and nobody could run as fast as he. Then he ran home to his mother, hopping and skipping, on his own fleet furry toes, for he vowed that never again would he wear any slippers.

The Brook's Secret

Somewhere in England there is a long steep field, with oak trees and hawthorns growing round the borders, and foxglove and dog-roses standing purple and pink under the walls. Down the middle runs a wild little brook, which is in such a hurry you can scarcely hear what it says. But all the time it calls, 'A secret! A secret! A secret!'

I found out the secret, and here it is.

Near the brook once stood a tiny green house. It had a roof of green rushes, two lattice windows, one up and one down, and a brown door. The door-knocker was a hawthorn berry, and the door-mat a thistle flower, which, as you know, is a soft white brush, just right for small muddy feet.

At the back was a narrow window which was upstairs, yet level with the ground, for the field was so steep one could step out from the wee bedroom on to the grassy slope.

In this pretty house lived a frog. He was a good-natured little fellow, with bright eyes and cheerful manners.

He played the flute, and every evening he could be heard piping away, or singing with his croaky voice as he sat by the front door looking out at the stream, or as he leaned from his bedroom window peeping up the field at the foxgloves.

One day he saw something in the grass on the hillside, something strange, like a bit of sky fallen to the ground. He fetched his spy-glass, which was a bulrush stem, and peered again from his back window. Then he went up the hill with his cherry-wood stick in his hand, hopping and skipping, panting and excited, to get a nearer look.

Whatever could it be, this exquisite creature? There she lay, half hidden by the buttercups and daisies, a fairy girl with golden hair and a dress of blue gauze!

The frog was filled with delight as he gazed at her. He made a litter of cunningly woven leaves, and carried her carefully home. He touched her tiny curved fingers, and spoke gently to her in his husky whisper.

But she never answered; she smiled and smiled, so that he knew she was happy, but never a word did she utter. He laid her on a bed of sheep's wool, which he had plucked from the brambles, and she shut her blue eyes and slept. He roused her, and lifted her to a chair of bracken fronds, and she opened her wonderful eyes again.

The frog was enraptured. He sat by this delicate lady, and played his little flute to her. But

although she never failed to reward him with a smile, she never spoke a word.

'She must be hungry,' said he, and he put fresh watercress, duckweed and groundsel before her, but she never ate. He picked round pearly mushrooms from the meadows, and berries, and seeds of sweet plants, and made salads of burnet and sorrel and thyme, but she only smiled.

He even brought an egg from the farmyard, rolling it downhill, pushing it uphill, until he got it, all green with grass stains, to her side. But she never even glanced at it.

The little frog loved her dearly, for she was so beautiful. He had never seen anyone like her before. He put daisies in her flaxen hair, and forget-me-nots in her pale hands, but her fixed smile never changed.

'She must be bewitched by the elves,' groaned the frog, and he played a sad little tune on his flute.

Then one day he shut the front door and locked it, and put the key under the thistle flower.

He travelled down the stream, past fields of long waving grass, and ponds fringed with rushes, past rough little pastures where young colts played, and under great trees which dipped their branches into the brook – by now considerably bigger.

He left the friendly stream and turned to the right, along a tiny narrow path which only the sharpest eyes could spy. It led to a garden of purple orchis, and in the midst was a house, much larger than the frog's, solid and strong, the house of a wise old toad. He was so old, a hundred years at least, he must know everything.

The frog knocked at the toad's door, and a little maid answered.

'Is Mr Toad at home?' asked the frog politely.

'What is your name?' asked the maid, with her green cap askew and her streamers dangling over her eyes, for she was one of those freckled brown frogs who never can keep tidy.

'Oh, just say it's a frog from the brook, on urgent business, but he wouldn't mind waiting a day or two in this garden, if it isn't convenient to Mr Toad,' said the frog, and the little maid took the message.

Frog was shown into the great toad's study, which was lined with books on flowers and herbs, on butterflies and moths, on stars and weather and winds.

'Pardon my intrusion,' said the frog timidly to the wise animal, 'but I want the advice of the wisest one, and so I came to you, Mr Toad.'

Toad nodded.

'I love an enchanted being, the fairest of the fair, with a smiling face and eyes that open and shut. But she never speaks or moves or drinks or eats or sings or walks.'

Toad looked interested. 'Where did she come

from?' he asked.

'I found her lying in my field, among the buttercups and daisies,' answered the frog.

Toad went to his bookshelf, and hunted among the books on butterflies and moths, but she wasn't there. He took down the books on animals, but there was nothing like her. He searched among the books on fairies and elves, but although these were fair, they had not the smiles of the little person whom Frog had found.

Then Toad took down a book on children.

'It may be in here,' said he, turning the pages rapidly with his fat thumbs. The frog leaned over, and had flying visions of humming-tops and marbles, of bows and arrows, rattles and balls. Then he saw a picture of a doll, just like his fairy creature.

'Stop! Stop! There she is!' he cried, excitedly.

'That's a doll, a toy used by children since Roman times,' said Toad, learnedly. 'Dolls were known in Ancient Egypt. In fact,' Toad went on, 'wherever there are children, there will dolls be found.'

'But I don't want children,' shuddered the frog, 'I want the enchantment taken off my friend, so that she can listen to my flute-playing, and share my green house by the brook, and walk in the steep field with me.'

'The wisest Toad can tell you what to do, if you only have patience, and don't interrupt,' said

Toad severely. He shut the book, and put it carefully back on the shelf. Then he sat down on the scarlet toadstooi which grew in the middle of the study floor, and addressed the frog, who sat humbly beneath its shaodw.

'You must put the flowers of eye-bright, the little white speckledy flower which grows in the old quarry, on her eyes, so that they will recognize you. You must put mouse-ear, that silky leaf which grows in dry places, on her ears, so that she will hear you. You must put hare's-foot, that soft grass which grows in the meadows, on her feet, so that she can run. You must put heart's-ease, that tiny yellow pansy, which grows in the short grass of the high pastures, on her heart. Then let her lie on a bed of quicken boughs from the hedge, and she will awake. This was taught to my ancestors by an old Hermit long ago, when the world was much younger than it is today.'

The grateful frog hurried home, not stopping to watch the trees dipping in the water, or the swallows flying over the fields. He picked the flowers of eye-bright, and heart's-ease, the mouse-ear, and hare's-foot, and the twigs from the quickset hedge. He followed Toad's directions, and laid the small doll among the herbs and grasses.

When she felt the magic plants about her, she sat up and looked around. Then she laughed so that dimples came in her cheeks, and she leapt to her feet. She danced round the little room, holding out her blue gauze skirts with her curving fingers, fluttering round the fascinated frog like a butterfly.

She tasted the watercress, and the sweet berries the frog had provided, and drank fresh water from the brook. She ran in the fields, and leapt among the flowers.

So the frog and the doll lived together, the greatest of friends, for many years in the little green house by the brook. When they visited the toad, they took a jar of honey and a yellow cloak of toad-flax, which the doll had woven for his old age, and they looked at his wonderful books while he tasted their sweets.

But the nicest time of all was twilight, when the evening star came out, and they sat on the stools of mushrooms, the frog playing merry tunes on his flute, the doll singing softly in a tiny voice.

And there she may be now, for she was as happy as a bee the last time I saw her, peeping from her window at the back of the little green thatched house by the brook. But only the brook and I know exactly where it is.

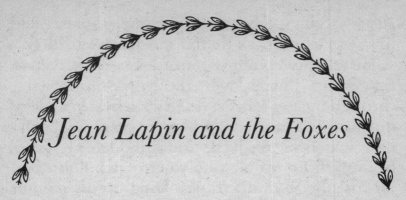

Jean Lapin and the Foxes

As the shadows lengthened, and the sun sank below the distant hills, the peace of the countryside was broken by a rumbling noise. Little Jack Rabbit threw down the basket in which he had been gathering blackberries, and hid under the briars, with his eyes fixed on the empty house on the edge of the Common.

It had been vacant ever since he could remember, and cobwebs hung over the dark windows, screening the inside from young inquisitive eyes. Toadstools and nettles grew in the garden, instead of flowers, and gooseberry bushes and damson trees were half wild.

A furniture-van drove up, and some very queer things came out of it. First a sharp-featured gentleman climbed down, and his wife followed, peering this way and that at the scenery, nodding her head at the Common with the little group of rabbit cottages. They dragged out the oddest collection of furniture – a medley of chairs and old bedsteads, three-legged tables, cracked jugs, and

109

rusty frying-pans, and the most miserable blankets. Even Jack Rabbit saw they were dirty.

He was just coming out to ask if he could help to carry the things over the gorse-bushes and through the nettlebeds, when he hesitated and lay quite still. There was a strange scent about the pair which he disliked, and although he was a friendly little rabbit who would fetch and carry for anyone, he waited, wrinkling up his nose in disgust. Really it made his hair stand on end! How could they use such stuff! Was it the hair-oil they used — for their tails were trim and well-brushed — or was it soap?

'I won't help them, but I'll send them a bottle of lavender water,' said he to himself, and when the door of the old house was shut, he ran home.

'Mother, Mother,' he cried, tumbling in at the doorway. 'Someone's come to live in the empty house on Common Edge, by the gorse-bushes, you know.'

'I hope they are nice people,' said Mrs Rabbit, as she put away her ironing. 'The last who lived there were most undesirable. Most undesirable,' and she shook her head sadly. 'It was before you were born; I was only young myself. He was a hunter, but he came to a bad end — met a game-keeper, I heard.'

'This is a red-whiskered gentleman and his wife,' said Jack Rabbit. 'They brought a van full of furniture, so they are going to stay a long time.'

'I wonder who they are,' mused Mrs Rabbit. 'They may be some relations of the Squirrels.'

'They use horrible scent, Mother, and I want to give them a bottle of your lavender water. May I?'

Mrs Rabbit started.

'A scent?' she cried. 'Red-whiskered and scented? It cannot be the Foxes, surely? They would never dare to come to live so near the Common!'

'The Bogey-Man!' exclaimed Jack Rabbit, delighted. Ever since he was a baby he had been told, 'The Fox will catch you if you are not good,' and now here was the very animal! He chuckled with glee, but Mrs Rabbit was alarmed.

'I will first make sure, and if it is the Foxes, you must never, never go near, for' – and here she lowered her voice to a whisper – 'they will eat you if they catch you.'

Little Jack Rabbit stared. 'Eat me? Eat my ears and my nose and my paws?' he cried.

'Yes, eat you all up, so that there is nothing left at all,' replied Mrs Rabbit, sternly.

'Eat my tail, too?' persisted Jack Rabbit.

'Of course, child,' said Mrs Rabbit impatiently; she reached for her jacket and hat, and went out.

She tripped softly along the little green path, scarcely moving the daisies with her small feet as she pattered along. At a clump of flowering gorse she halted and peered through the prickles.

There was the uninhabited house, with smoke

111

curling from the chimney, and the empty furniture-van at the door. She saw Mrs Fox pay the driver and then enter the house.

The rabbit went sadly home.

'We must move,' she told her husband that night, as they sat in their rocking-chairs talking over the new neighbours.

'There will be no peace now on the Common, no jolly rambles by moonlight, and mushroom picnics at dawn. Nobody will come to supper with us, if they have to return past the Foxes' house. It wouldn't be safe! No, we must find another house.'

She cried softly as she thought of her cupboards and shelves, her fine larder, and the pretty garden full of harebells and clover. Little Jack Rabbit lay awake, listening, and he clenched his small fist as he thought of the house on the Common.

Next day Mr Rabbit went off to explore the country at the other side of the river, but houses were few, and there was no place like his own home. Mrs Rabbit began to pack her china in little wooden boxes, and Jack Rabbit ran backwards and forwards helping her.

In every cottage on the Common it was the same. All the rabbits hurriedly collected their goods, and borrowed paper and string from each other. The old rabbits shook their heads sadly, but the young ones jumped with joy, for they thought all change was an adventure.

Only little Jack Rabbit of all the young ones

was sorry to go, but he called together a band of friends and talked it over.

'Why not make the Foxes leave the district?' he said. 'We were here first.'

'Let's write him a letter,' said one.

'Who will deliver it?' asked a very small rabbit.

'Send it by Magpie. He dare go anywhere.'

So they wrote a letter, printing it on a dock leaf in large writing:

'GO AWAY AT ONCE. DANGER. TRESPASSERS WILL BE PROSECUTED. SIGNED BY ORDER. JEAN LAPIN.'

It was Jack Rabbit's idea to sign it in French, so that the Foxes would be mystified, for he had learned a few words from the swallows, who had picked up a smattering on their way across from Africa.

The Magpie pushed the letter under the door of the old house, and Mrs Fox found it.

'Hello! What's this? An invitation?' and she tore open the envelope. Mr Fox leaned over her shoulder as she read it.

'Trespassers will be prosecuted,' she read. 'That's what it said in the wood where the traps were laid, and the gamekeeper lived. It's a warning! Who is this Jean Lapin? Some French Fox who wants to warn us?'

The Foxes felt nervous as they walked round their garden and gazed across the country at the woods beyond the Common.

'Is it a gun or a trap I must avoid?' said Mr Fox,

and he stepped gingerly through his gate and walked across the grass.

The rabbits were all in their holes, parcelling up their story-books which they read on winter nights, wrapping up their cups and saucers, folding blankets and eiderdowns.

The Fox saw no one, but a pair of eyes watched him until he went out of sight.

Jack Rabbit picked some broad green grasses, which grew by the stream, and then he searched until he had found a piece of chalk.

He trotted across the Common, and lay under the gorse bushes, waiting until Mrs Fox came out. She sat in the garden knitting, so Jack Rabbit crept up to the back door. With the chalk he drew a skull and cross-bones. Then he climbed up on the roof and sat behind the chimney.

Soon Mr Fox came home, empty-handed, and Mrs Fox joined him. He had seen never a rabbit, and he had been scared of traps and guns. He was in a thoroughly bad temper, and he stamped round to the back to wipe his boots.

He started when he saw the drawing on the door, and Mrs Fox burst into tears. They pushed open the door, half expecting to see somebody there, and then bolted it.

Jack Rabbit held the grasses across his long front teeth and blew with all his might, so that his cheeks stood out like balloons. A horrible squeaking and howling came down the chimney.

'What's that?' cried Mr Fox, leaping up in a fright.

'It's perhaps a hyena,' sobbed Mrs Fox.

They opened the door and peeped about. The little rabbit skipped round the chimney, and they saw no one, so they returned to the house to talk it over.

Jack Rabbit slipped softly down, and ran away as fast as he could go.

The Foxes made up the fire and sat down again.

'It was only the wind in the chimney,' said Mr Fox, to pacify his wife.

But Jack Rabbit returned with a hollow bone.

'Oo-oo-oo-oo-oo,' he called into the bone, and 'Oo-oo-oo-oo-oo,' came moaning down the chimney.

'Goodness, whatever's that?' cried the Foxes, springing up like a pair of Jack-in-the-boxes.

'Oo-oo-oo-oo-oo,' filled the room, as the rabbit boomed into the bone.

The Foxes dashed to the door, but nothing was to be seen except the stars shining in the sky.

They shivered and went back to the house.

'Was it a lion, do you think?' cried Mrs Fox, shaking and shivering.

'It was only the wind in the chimney,' said Mr Fox again.

But Jack Rabbit slipped down and ran across the Common to a turnip field. He picked a large pink turnip and scraped out the inside, which he ate. He scooped and hollowed until he had made a rabbit face, with eyes and widely open mouth.

He fetched a candle from his home, and put it inside. Then he carried and trundled it to the Foxes' house. He lighted the candle with a bit of flint and tinder, and stuck it on a hazel wand.

Then he leaned it against the uncurtained window.

'Oo-oo-oo-oo-oo,' he called down the chimney again.

The Foxes who were dozing, awoke, and saw the turnip rabbit shining through the cobwebs at the window, with two glaring eyes, and a wide open mouth.

Their last bit of courage fled, and they dashed through the door, with a yell.

Away they went, across the Common, through the wood, over hill and stream, to the far country where the sun sets. They would never return for their sticks of furniture. They had had enough of that haunted house, with its strange noises and warnings.

All the rabbits untied their parcels, unwrapped their blankets, remade their beds, and settled down again, thankful to be rid of their unwelcome neighbour. They invited Jack Rabbit to a moonlight celebration, and they danced round a turnip lantern which Jack stuck in a gorse bush near the old house. A couple of Bats came to live there, but no one was afraid of *them*.

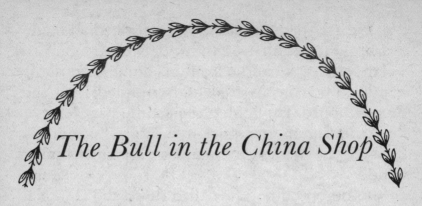

The Bull in the China Shop

Miss Tabitha Timpitty kept a very fine china shop in the village of Liedown, which is four miles South of East of Bedford. She sold cups and saucers, dishes and plates, babies' mugs and grandmothers' jugs, besides teapots of every size and colour. There was a gold teapot wreathed in roses for a Queen, a brown teapot with a leafy handle for a mother, a blue teapot with a football on the lid for a little boy, and a pink teapot as big as a walnut for a doll. People came from far and near to buy china from Miss Tabitha.

But one day she ate a green apple, and it gave her such a pain she had to go to bed, so there was no one to mind the shop. She called her Pussy-cat, Tibby, to her, as she lay moaning and groaning in her four-poster bed.

'Tibby, dear, I want you – Oh, Oh – I want you – Oh, Oh – to mind the shop for me.'

'Yes, mistress, I will mind the shop for you,' mewed Tibby, giving her a pill.

She ran downstairs and sat on the counter. The

first person to enter was naughty Tommy Tittle-mouse, who wanted to buy a pie-dish.

Tibby said, 'What can I do for you, please?'

'You can let me pull your tail,' replied the boy, giving it a sharp twitch, which sent Tibby over the counter into a pile of plates.

Tommy seized a pie-dish and ran off without paying for it, but Tibby went upstairs crying and mewing to her mistress.

'Oh dear! Oh dear!' exclaimed Miss Tabitha Timpitty. 'I must get someone else to mind my shop. Do go out and find somebody, Tibby dear, somebody stronger than you.'

Tibby ran out of the room and slid down the banisters to the shop. She stepped out into the street, but a dog saw her and gave chase. Up a tree she scurried, and from a safe branch she called down, 'If you leave me alone and go to Miss Tabitha Timpitty, at the china shop, you will hear some good news.'

The dog scampered off, dashed into the shop, upsetting a dinner-service, and barked loudly to Miss Tabitha.

'Bow-wow. What is it you want, please?'

'If you will mind my shop for me, you shall have a juicy bone,' called Miss Tabitha from her bedroom.

'That I will,' said the dog, as he lay down by the counter.

A few minutes later Tommy came in for a milk

jug.

'What can I do for you, please?' asked the dog politely.

'You can let me pull your tail,' shouted the boy, giving such a pull that the dog fell on the pile of plates, and ran howling from the shop.

'Oh dear! Oh dear!' cried Miss Tabitha, shivering as she heard the noise. 'Tibby, Tibby, you must go out and find someone wiser.'

So Tibby, who had crept upstairs again, slid down the banisters and ran out of the shop.

Just then there passed a flock of sheep.

'These are bigger than the dog,' thought Tibby. 'I will get one of them to mind my mistress's shop.'

'Hello, there,' she called to a large white sheep which was running ahead of the others. 'Stop, stop. Wait a minute, Mrs Sheep, I have some good news for you. Miss Tabitha Timpitty wants you in her china shop.'

The sheep turned into the shop, and ran to the foot of the stairs, but all the rest of the sheep followed after, and there was such a bleating and baa-ing, and breaking of pots, Miss Tabitha burst into tears.

Tibby and the big sheep managed to send the flock away, but the floor was covered with fragments of china.

'What is it you want?' called the sheep upstairs to Miss Tabitha.

'If you will mind my shop for me,' sobbed Miss Tabitha, 'you shall have a dish of turnips.'

'That I will,' replied the sheep, as she stood among the wreckage.

Just then Tommy came into the shop to buy a teapot.

'What can I do for you, please?' asked the sheep.

'You can let me pull your tail,' said Tommy, giving her such a tug she ran out of the shop and never stopped until she found the flock. But Tommy grabbed the teapot, and ran off without paying.

'Oh dear! Oh dear! Tibby, you must find someone better than that,' sighed Miss Tabitha.

So Tibby ran out of the room, slid down the banisters, and went into the street.

A bull was passing on its way to the butcher's.

'He is bigger than the sheep; I will get him to mind my mistress's shop.'

So she called, 'Mr Bull, Mr Bull, can you spare me a minute? Miss Tabitha wants to speak to you.'

'Spare a minute?' asked the bull. 'I can spare you days and weeks and years.'

He stepped into the shop, lifting his hooves high over the broken pots, and walked softly to the foot of the stairs.

'What is it you want, Miss Tabitha?' he asked. 'I am on the way to the butcher, and he is waiting

for me.'

'If you will mind my shop for me,' said Miss Tabitha, 'he can wait for ever.'

'That I will,' said the bull, 'with all my heart.'

He found a broom, and swept up the floor. Then he dusted the shelves of china, and arranged the teapots on a table. He moved so softly Miss Tabitha heard no sound, but Tibby sat watching round the corner of the room.

When he had finished, he lay down behind the counter, with only the bushy tip of his tail showing.

Soon naughty Tommy came back, carrying a clothes-basket.

'What can I do for you, please?' mooed the bull, softly as a dove, for he was anxious to please Miss Tabitha.

'You can let me pull your tail,' said Tommy, pulling at the tuft, and preparing to run off with a load of china.

Then up jumped the bull, and with a roar he lowered his head and tossed the boy and his clothes-basket out of the shop, over the houses, into a pond.

The villagers ran to their doors when they heard the roar, and saw the boy flying through the air.

'There goes Tommy, bad Tommy,' they cried, 'Miss Tabitha has at last thrown him out of her shop. Well, even a worm will turn!'

They went to the shop to thank Miss Tabitha. Behind the counter sat the bull, wearing a white apron, and polishing the glass dishes with a cloth.

'What can I do for you, please?' he asked, cooing softly as a wood-pigeion. 'I have a fine collection of teapots over here.'

So each woman bought a teapot, and returned with a friend for another. All day the bull was busy selling china and wrapping it up. Even the butcher's wife bought a stewpot, but she vowed she would keep it for vegetables only.

Miss Tabitha was so pleased with his delicate air, yet manly strength, she kept him as her assistant, and people came thick and fast to see the bull in the china shop.

Patricia Cleveland-Peck
The String Family 95p

The miniature world of the String family – Mr and Mrs String, their children,
Hemp, Flax, Twine and baby Skein all come alive and share their
adventures with Sally in Miss Floribunda's cottage in the country. Sally is
the only human child to be introduced to the String family and friends – a
wonderland of aunts and cousins with exciting and exotic names – the
Binder-Twines, the Garden-Lines and the Embroidery-Silks.

The String Family in Summer £1.00

The String Family live very happily amongst the old-fashioned dinner
service on top of the dresser which belongs to Miss Floribunda, the owner
of Willow Cottage. Mr and Mrs String have their work cut out preventing
their lively children – Hemp, Flax, Twine and baby Skein – from being tied
up in knots! They also have to cope with a variety of aunts and cousins who
all have exotic-sounding names – the Binder-Twines, the Garden-Lines,
and the Embroidery-Silks!

Ann Lawrence
Oggy and the Holiday 90p

Both Oggy the hedgehog and Tiggy the kitten enjoy the new experience of a seaside holiday where they meet some new and interesting friends.

All good things must come to an end – the friends say goodbye – but somehow Oggy gets left behind . . .

The Travels of Oggy 95p

Oggy is a young unadventurous hedgehog who lives very happily in a garden near Hampstead Heath which belongs to 'his' family. But when his family move to the country, Oggy gets lonely and decides to follow them . . .

Colin Dann
The Animals of Farthing Wood £2.50

Farthing Wood is threatened . . . Man is moving in with bulldozers. The
animals are desperate, their homes are destroyed and their very survival is
at stake. Can they escape? Will fox and badger lead them to the safety of a
new home? The journey is difficult and dangerous . . . can fox and badger
keep the animals together? Will they all survive to find peace and
happiness?

All these books are available at your local bookshop or newsagent, or can be ordered
direct from the publisher. Indicate the number of copies required and fill in the form
below

....

Name ————————————————————————————————
(Block letters please)

Address————————————————————————————————

————————————————————————————————————

Send to CS Department, Pan Books Ltd,
PO Box 40, Basingstoke, Hants
Please enclose remittance to the value of the cover price plus:
35p for the first book plus 15p per copy for each additional book
ordered to a maximum charge of £1.25 to cover postage and
packing
Applicable only in the UK

While every effort is made to keep prices low, it is sometimes
necessary to increase prices at short notice. Pan Books reserve the
right to show on covers and charge new retail prices which may
differ from those advertised in the text or elsewhere